*f*P

ALSO BY BENILDE LITTLE

Good Hair
The Itch

ACTING OUT

BENILDE LITTLE

A Novel

THE FREE PRESS

NEW YORK   LONDON   TORONTO
SYDNEY   SINGAPORE

*f*P

THE FREE PRESS
A Division of Simon & Schuster Inc.
1230 Avenue of the Americas
New York, NY 10020

THE FREE PRESS and colophon are
trademarks of Simon & Schuster, Inc.

Designed by Jan Pisciotta

Manufactured in the United States of America

ISBN 0-684-85480-5

For Baldwin and Ford

When we are alone and quiet we are afraid that something will be whispered in our ear, and so we hate the silence and drug ourselves with social life.

—NIETZSCHE

What a relief it is when we stop trying to be something and become someone.

—COCO CHANEL

Author's Note

While Eleazer is an actual family name, these characters and situations are creations born in my imagination, as are the characters in all my other books. Some names like Eleazer, like Stone Ridge Country Day School of the Sacred Heart (thanks, Lori Millen), are better than anything I could make up.

Thank you for allowing my imaginary world to enter yours. Hope you enjoy.

Acknowledgments

All of my work is pulled from places inside my imagination and my soul. My friends, often unknowingly, act as midwives who listen, talk, entertain my children, bring me food, read my work and, most importantly, give me love. Thank you—Sharon Joan Brown, Wendy Rountree, Eleanore Wells, Valerie Wilson Wesley, Iqua Colson, Stephanie Stokes Oliver, Lynne Toye, Christina Baker Kline, Alice Elliott Dark, Monique and Glenn Greenwood Pogue, Linda Villarosa, Tanya Carter Barnes, Elizabeth Branson, Connie Thames, Sheila Baynes, and Hillary Jaffe Reimnitz. Thanks, Susan Herman.

Thanks to the people who have taken care of my babies: Rose Powell, Remi Gill, Malvin Wray, Beth Respess and the original, Dawn McClean; the amazing grandparents, Clara and Matthew Little and Joan and Clifford Virgin.

Thanks, again, to my agent and friend the sublime Faith Hampton Childs and to my stellar editor and human being Dominick Anfuso. To Carolyn Reidy, Martha Levin, Suzanne Donahue, Sue Flemming, Carissa Hays, Sara Schneider, and the Simon & Schuster sales and marketing team—thanks for going to the mat for my work.

A gigantic thanks to my husband, my partner, Cliff Virgin, who every day makes me believe.

PART I

Sucker Punched

CHAPTER ONE

When I married Jay I was sure he'd never leave me. I was certain that he loved me more and that he loved the life we'd made together. If anyone was going to do the leaving it was going to be me. I'm convinced I thought about it more than he did—looking at my softening face in the mirror as I sat in the beauty salon; sitting in the car wash tempted to open the window and let in that nasty soapy water inside the white Range Rover he'd insisted on buying; strolling down the aisle of Grant's mindlessly putting butter, eggs, cereal, and ground turkey in the cart. I'd imagine myself going home, setting the groceries on the kitchen floor and leaving. The idea rolled around my head like a pebble in my shoe. Too big to ignore, but eventually I did and the feeling went away, or I should tell you I made it go away. I deaden those feelings with my will and when that stalled I ingested a little blue pill. The pill also rid me of those knavish thoughts that took up residence in my mind for as long as I can remember. The pill let me let go.

Jay had wanted, and he literally said this, a real family that would look good in the Christmas card. Why hadn't I just packed up when he said that? He had actually considered the vision of red plaid-donned children on a damn Christmas card important. Jay was a good father, but I was the one in charge of the reality of three kids—the daily doling out of hugs, support, information, monitoring homework, scheduling doctor appointments, play dates, lessons, teacher conferences and on and on and on. But now he has left me and I hate feeling like a damn cliché, but I am, we are. He left me, I'd later learned, for a younger, thinner, better-credentialed woman who he'd met at a traffic light. I'd become the aging suburban housewife who wore jeans six days out of seven and lived my life inside the demands of a carpool. But I wasn't frumpy or unattractive, although like most I'd gained an extra few pounds with each kid, which now amounted to ten to fifteen that I could stand to lose. I dressed the way that was appropriate for the kind of life I lived—shuttling kids, taking care of a baby and a house and cooking and organizing all of our lives. That's what I did.

I didn't start out wanting the kind of life we ended up having. I had wanted to own my life, but that concept was amorphous, and then I got hurt and scared and there was Jay who knew exactly what he wanted and said he wanted me to be with him, so I figured why not. I knew he knew what he wanted to do and maybe along the way I'd figure out how to live the life I wanted. My instinct had told me that I needed to marry myself first, cleave to a clearly defined self first, but Jay was nice enough, successful enough, handsome enough, good enough in bed, my friends liked him enough and I remember thinking, during the rehearsal dinner, This is enough. There was some wow to have found this person who is right for me, even if I didn't quite know what that was. He's good enough. I didn't listen to myself back then—I was twenty-six and self-knowledge was still more than a decade away. What I did know about myself scared me. I knew I didn't want to be like the women who came before me—my mother and grandmother and aunts—wild, untamable women who at one time were fierce and lively but seemed to practice a kind of antilove. They were vivid, hard and often joyless. They scared the shit out of me. What I convinced myself of was that I wanted to be sedate and reserved, which I'd decided was normal, and to let someone else worry about personhood.

Jay's work, or I should say success, allowed me to not have to work and the freedom to volunteer on the PTA, work out, see my friends for lunch and shop. I shopped when I was happy and when I was not. I shopped for me, for my kids, their friends, the house, my friends' houses. I had been happy enough. Happier than I'd been in my own birth family—where my mother was never home and when she was, she was only happy in our garage, which was her studio, covered in paint and working on a canvas. She had had a passion that didn't have anything to do with my father or me. She was frustrated by a lack of creative opportunity and had never settled in her work as a high school art teacher, but still labored in that garage long after she stopped showing or being represented. She had artist and writer and musician friends who we didn't know well, who she seemed to need to breathe. She'd leave for days at a time, leaving Daddy in charge of braiding my hair, helping me with my schoolwork and Girl Scout projects, all the things mothers and daughters were suppose to do. Daddy loved my mother with a childlike devotion. He used to say he had three things in his life that mattered: running—he'd been a sprinter in college who became a high school gym teacher, my mother and me. I believed the running was a distant second to Mother and I came in, maybe, third. It didn't really matter, though, because I wanted my mother to help me with my homework and my Girl Scout projects and to do my hair. When I was pregnant with Malcolm, it was my dad who called up some friends and hosted a shower for me. When I had Malcolm I thanked God that I'd had a boy and wouldn't have to deal with a daughter who'd force me to deal with all the anger and lack I'd had with my own mother. Then I had another boy and I took that as a sign of God's grace. Then one night after one of Paula Sweet's perfect dinner parties and me having too much wine, which was the only way I got through them, Jay and I came home, fell into bed without my diaphragm. We made Ivy and I seriously considered getting rid of it. If RU486 had been available I'm sure I would have. Then I found out that it was a girl and spent the rest of my pregnancy petrified, although some part of me knew I needed to deal with my mother issues. I named her Ivy because it is strong, constantly growing and resilient, my hope for her.

Ivy was five months old, I was feeding her rice cereal mixed with breast milk when Jay said he was leaving me. Cereal was on her fingers and face and in both of our hair. She was in her high chair laughing and I felt unrestrained happiness only a baby's laughter can provide. Even with breast milk running down my T-shirt and onto my overalls, and cereal on the red bandanna that was supposed to hold up my hair, I felt glamorous. I often did, in my jeans or overalls or khakis, like I was one of those cool stay-at-home moms you see in computer ads. I didn't understand feeling unattractive, like I overheard other women at my kids' school complain about. My body and hair were in good enough shape and my makeup was in some evidence. I had to keep reminding myself that I would be forty on my next birthday. Of course, I didn't look like the women, I should say girls, in fashion magazines, or the ones who Jay worked with, those real estate women who drove Mercedes wagons, wore gold Rolexes with diamonds, got their hair blown out twice a week and were acquainted with Botox. But I didn't want to look like maintaining my looks was my job.

Jay walks in, through the back door that was always unlocked. It was too early for him to be home for lunch, but not unusual for him to drop by the house during the day if he was working out of his Pomona office. A year ago, he'd set up an office in Harlem, and in this hot market his workload had doubled. He checked the mail, which sat as it always did in a basket on the granite kitchen counter, grunted something about his shirts having been delivered, went and got them from the hall closet and then, as if he'd asked "what's for dinner?" said, "I'm leaving you." Just like that. No "we've got to talk" or "I've been thinking" or even "you know I'm not really happy." Nothing. Just I'm leaving you. I sat there for a moment, still feeding Ivy, thinking, I think he just said I'm leaving you, but telling myself, No, you're wrong, he couldn't have said that, what are you, crazy? He can't leave you; you have kids, three kids, a mortgage, an SUV and a station wagon and a swim club membership. I put the tiny rubber-tipped spoon down in to one of the two sections of the peach-colored plastic bowl and turned around to look at Jay's face. It was clinched and stern and I couldn't tell whether he was trying to hold back tears or if he was furious and trying not to show it.

"What did you say?"

He looked down and started babbling about life being a one-shot deal and having to make the most of it and being back in the city . . . and . . . lonely . . . and then my ears stopped working and I thought, well, I'll stand up—maybe if he sees me, he'll snap out of this lunacy. He'll see me and Ivy and he'll snap out of it.

"Jay, Jay, Jay. Wait. What? What're you trying to say? What's this? What are you talking about?"

I touched his forearm and he stepped away from me. He rubbed his eye with one hand, exhaled in what seemed to be frustration.

"I'm just not happy anymore, Ina. I haven't been for a long time and it's just, I think better, it'll be better like this. I can't, I just can't keep this going."

"Keep what going?"

He blew out again, this time seeming less certain of his position.

"This," he said and looked up, his hands up, waving toward the ceiling. "All this. I just don't want this anymore."

"Okay, so all what? What's wrong?"

He practically whispered, "I don't know you anymore."

He looked at me and quickly looked away. "You're not who I married." He opened the door and walked out. Just like that, just like he had every morning for the past thirteen years. He just walked out. Now Ivy was chanting "Da-Da . . . Da-Da . . . Da-Da." The only word she says. They all say it first, Mama, Mommy comes way later, a year sometimes. A more complicated and deeper expression, I guess, takes more time to master. Once they do, of course, you wish they didn't because they must say it six-hundred times a day. My head felt like someone was standing on it. I wanted to go upstairs and get into my big, feathered bed, feel the smooth 380-thread count sheets against my body, the goose down on top of me and under my head. I needed a nap; I needed to sleep like Aurora, only longer, like Rip Van Winkle. I need to sleep so long that when I wake up all the pain, all the explaining, the messes, the fights, the bouts of self-loathing that will come, would be over.

I called my neighbor Paige to watch Ivy and maybe even the boys when they got home from school. She had four kids, her three younger ones around the same ages as mine. She had an au pair and a live-in housekeeper. It was never a problem having three more kids in her large, rambling house. I gathered Ivy out of her high chair, wiped cereal from her hair, face and hands with a wet paper towel, put her socks back on, pulled on a knit hat and sweater and carried her next door. My neighbor was in her kitchen watching the Food Network on her wide-screen TV that was built into a wall; she was cooking along with the TV and talking on the phone. She waved a wooden spoon at me and Ingracia appeared, as if summoned by spoon, and took Ivy from my arms.

"Gracias," I said to her and smiled. She smiled back and immediately began removing Ivy's hat and sweater while cooing to her.

My neighbor got off the phone and said, in her usual sarcastic way, "You look great! Big party tonight?"

I just breathed in and out deeply and thanked her for rescuing me, again.

"I'm exhausted. I've gotta lay down."

"Go, get some rest. You know we love having her. You want the boys to come here after school?"

"Malcolm and Marcus'll be home around five, after soccer practice . . ."

"Fine, I'll look out for them. They like meatloaf? That's what the kids are having."

"Yeah, that'll be fine. I need to lie down. My head is . . ."

"Go, go, and rest. If you don't feel any better later, they can just sleep over. We love having them, don't even think about it, go . . ."

My look hugged her and I hoped she could feel how totally, truly grateful I was.

"The back door'll be opened if they wanna come home," I said wearily as I left.

I let the screen door close behind me, scribbled on a Post-it and stuck it to the door, instructing the boys to go next door for dinner. I breathed in the silence of my house. I couldn't recall the last time it had been this quiet, when the last time was that I was alone in it. I used to love to be alone with my thoughts, daydreaming for hours as a child and then sharing some of it with my cousin Zackie, who would remain my confidant into adulthood, who'd listen to my dreams with his eyes closed, as if visualizing pictures of what I said.

It was fall and chillier inside than it was out. We hadn't turned the heat up yet. I went to the thermostat—it was at fifty-six degrees. I moved it to sixty-nine and looked around my family room. Every detail of this house I'd put my soul into making sure was just right. The khaki duck fabric on the sectional for family viewing of our large-screen TV, for which I had an armoire built; the perfect coral-colored chenille throw over Jay's brown leather arm chair; the ficus I'd nurtured since it was a baby bush. Our black-and-white family photos in gallery frames, shot and framed and hung by me just so, chronicling all the children through gummy drool stage to toddlerdom to school age. I knew women who complained about getting lost in taking care of everyone but themselves, but I didn't feel that way. It was the common lament of the women who made up the mommy's group I'd been in when we lived in Brooklyn, when Malcolm was a baby. All the women were powerful used-to-bes: a banker, several lawyers, a journalist, but I'd never really had a career to miss. My photographer's assistant days had been short-lived. Of course, I would come to see I did give up something, but that'd come later.

Wasn't my book club, my volunteer work, shopping, something? I had things to do; I had a life, didn't I?

CHAPTER

TWO

The first thing I needed to do was change the sheets to get rid of the smell of his cologne, the one I had always thought of as "too much." I never liked guys who wore cologne, seemed too peacocky to me. It was one of the many things I disregarded about my tastes in men when I married Jay. I grabbed the box of breast pads and stuffed two new ones inside my bra. I took off my bandanna and overalls and jumped into my feathered cocoon. I closed my eyes, waited for sleep to sweep me away as it always did as soon as my head released into the pillow. But I was cold and couldn't get comfortable. I tossed and turned, hearing over and over, "You're not who I married." And even though I knew what I'd just witnessed was real I couldn't make myself believe it was. Jay was not the type to leave. He'd loved me. He loved our kids. He had everything he ever wanted. I was the one with unfulfilled ambition, the life of soccer practice and kids' birthday parties. He was in the world and had a refuge that I worked my ass off to create. What was the point of leaving? If it was for another woman, he should've known me well enough to know that I would've looked the other way. I really didn't care enough to end my marriage over a piece of pussy. Oh God. I sat upright in the bed, my eyes wide in discovery. Maybe this is about another woman. Maybe Jay has fallen in love with someone. Could he have been cheating and I didn't even notice? No, no way. I would've known. But would I? I flashed on all those nights late in Harlem. I never went there, never questioned anything he told me about his whereabouts. I was too exhausted. Jay wasn't the cheating kind and if he did, he was much too cautious to get in too deep. He's just trippin', he's under too much stress. This Harlem thing has been too much for him to handle. I'm not the same person he married. I inhaled deeply, forced myself to focus on my breath, convincing myself he'd be back home in a couple days and I lay down again and fell into a deep, delicious sleep.

I woke up to the feel of Malcolm's lips on my cheek and saying good-bye. I pulled the comforter over my shoulder and turned to my side before I realized that it was morning and that they were dressed and going off to school.

"I made our lunches, Ma," he yelled as he bounded down the stairs, Marcus at his heels.

"Where's Ivy?" I yelled.

"Next door."

The screen door slammed. I looked outside my bedroom window and saw the school bus opening its door to usher them inside. Brown baby-sitters looking bored, holding on to strollers where white children sat, waiting to be pushed somewhere; mothers in jeans bouncing toddlers on their hips, appearing happy if distracted; mothers, some fathers, holding commuter mugs of coffee, dressed in business clothes and seeming anxious before heading off for their own bus. I always thought I'd be one of them, not necessarily in the beautifully tailored suit, sensible shoes and briefcase, but going off to conquer a world that had nothing to do with apple juice or Barney. And I was one, for a moment, when I was in real estate with Jay when he first left his corporate real estate job to start his own firm. It now seems like a lifetime ago, me working, dancing to the often frustrating beat of nannies, feeling free and pulled and stressed and happy. I still remember my first clients, still exchange Christmas cards with a few. But I always felt fraudulent, like this wasn't my real life, just something I was playing at. I was good enough at it, people liked me, I worked hard, but I didn't have that sales instinct, the close-at-any-cost instinct that Jay has, that the gold-level producers have. If I thought a property was crap or overpriced, I'd say so. I'd be showing a house and a movie would be playing in my head about the people who lived there or the fireplace would suddenly look like a sunflower. I wasn't interested in the furnace, whether the stove was gas or electric, flooding possibilities, none of that. I lay back on my bed and breathed deep, partially a reflex from seeing the kids off to school. For a second I'd forgotten that today was not yesterday, that today my life was drastically different than the one before. I checked the caller ID on the phone that sat on my nightstand next to the lamp, the boxes of breast pads and tissues, to see if Jay had called. I was sure he was simply having some kind of breakdown, that this was temporary, that he'd be home for dinner today or tomorrow.

I dialed Paige to check on Ivy.

"She's fine. She's watching Teletubbies with Emily. Ingracia's getting ready to take them to the park—we have the double jog stroller—don't worry."

"Paige, I . . ."

"I know you appreciate it. You need some rest."

With that she hung up and I knew she meant it. I could leave Ivy there for a month and it would actually be fine.

I had to admit that I was worn out. I rarely slept more than a few hours a night, hadn't since I had kids. I guiltily admitted that it felt great to not have to do anything but lay here, nobody calling "Mommy!" or needing to be fed, read to, bathed, nursed, rocked. After a few more minutes of idleness, I realized that I was famished. I went downstairs and groggily put on a pot of water. I went outside in my robe and gathered the newspapers off the lawn. We got three papers a day, the local one, the real one, and a New York tabloid. I flipped through the real one, reading the leads of the front-page stories, thinking about how stupid it was to rate the presidential debates like they were a Yankees game. Who won, who lost. One is an idiot and the other one has to keep from calling him that, what a waste of time. More endless fighting in the Middle East, I wonder if I'll see peace there in my lifetime. A story about bariatric surgery for people so fat they can't go to the movies or tie their own shoes. The operation closes off their small intestines. I don't know, maybe I'm just harsh, but how about stop eating so much! Enough of this, I just want the dessert. I pour coffee into the press and reach for the tabloid, flipping past their attempt at covering the same news I just read in the real newspaper. I flip to the gossip pages and do what I always do, scan the pictures for the black faces, read those boldface names first and then . . . but something causes me to back up, to stop before going on to read about Jennifer Aniston and . . . "Real estate princess Julie Jarvis and boyfriend Jay Robinson . . . party. . . . Donald Trump and girlfriend Ricki . . . party for Jennifer Lopez's . . ." There was a picture of Jay and a tall woman who could've been Latin or Italian or Greek. The party was last night. The night of the day he left us. There must be some mistake. Jay with a girlfriend? When? How? I sat there while the whistle on the kettle screamed. I sat there while the phone rang. I sat there while the bell rang. I just sat there.

I'm not sure how I got through the next week. I had a lot of help from Paige and my dad. I knew Paige knew by now that Jay had left me, but she hadn't said anything. I just didn't have any words for what I felt, so I didn't try any. Paige was a yenta, knew everybody and most everybody's business—but she was good at keeping things to herself, often not even sharing with her husband, Andy. He was an heir to a furniture fortune and ran a not-for-profit arts program for city kids. Paige and Andy knew everyone. My dad, who loved nothing more than being Grandpa to my

children, especially the two boys, asked about Jay and I
lied, saying he was busy on a project. I just kept going. Of
course I burned the rice, missed the teacher's conference,
forgot to pay the dry cleaning bill. The worst was forget-
ting to make the Halloween costumes. All the good ones
were gone and Malcolm was doing what he always does,
trying to make me feel better.

"Don't worry about it, Ma, it's no big deal. We'll find
something."

God, he was a great kid.

I still hadn't told them anything more than Daddy's on
business; Daddy's really busy in Harlem; Daddy took an
apartment in New York 'cause it's more convenient.

Eventually I knew I'd have to tell them, but I just
couldn't right now.

Jay is off with Julie Jarvis and left me with the mess of
having to deal with three kids.

Jay didn't call and check on us as he said he would and
when I tried to reach him on his cell I simply got his answering machine. I couldn't bring myself to leave a mes-
sage. What would I say? You short muthafucka, how dare
you? . . . Why didn't you just tell me you wanted to be with
someone else, you snake, you hypocrite, you piece of shit.
It just didn't seem like the kinds of things one says on an
answering machine. So I simmered and I smiled for my
kids and read their bedtime stories and played out our future in my head, imagining us having to move into a much
smaller house, maybe even an apartment, and having to

get a job because I'd refuse to take a dime from the slime Jay was. I knew I could find work if I had to, even if the kids would have to get used to much less. There are worse things. Oftentimes I felt like they had too damn much anyway and kids who grow up like that often don't amount to much, they have no drive. I wanted mine to strive for something, not to have everything laid at their feet, to be soft and lazy and assume that something was owed them.

In a way, I was one of those kids. We weren't rich and I didn't have everything I wanted, but I didn't want for much. We lived in a pristine yellow center hall colonial. It had deep green shutters and geraniums sprouting from window boxes that my father had built and then planted. My parents went into high gear when I came home from nursery school and announced that I was white. (Well, I didn't actually announce it; it was more like a pronouncement of *this is who I am.*) My mom tried to seem calm but was dying inside, trying to breathe after her lungs seemed to cease. But to my four-year-old self, white was normal, black was not, and I just wanted to be like everybody else—everybody who I knew at nursery school. After that they tried to do everything for me to make sure that I felt good about being black, or African-American as is now the "proper" term. I think it should be American-African or just American black since we're more American than anything else. They took me to see all the important black plays, black art exhibits, spent summers in an all-black beach colony, made sure all of their black friends had wonderful children for us to form wonderful, lifelong friendships with. They agree that I was the most agreeable child. I was an A student, I ran track, as my dad had, and basically did what I was told, whatever to just please my parents and keep them from stressing even more than they seemed to do naturally. I went to Howard 'cause they thought that would be good for me. A black college after my mostly white primary school years they thought would be a good antidote to becoming an Oreo, their great fear.

It was at Howard where I first encountered Jay. We were never formally introduced, didn't date or hang out in the same circle, but he was an outgoing, popular fraternity boy whose face I knew from around the yard. Jay also grew up in my hometown, Pomona, but on the other side, in a mostly black and working-class section called the Hollow. He was a small-town boy making good. His church paid his tuition, not that his mother wouldn't have mortgaged her soul to do so, but his church, his community was just that kind of place. At Howard he excelled in his business courses and gradually metamorphosed into AMID (A Man in Demand). Jay hung with the Greeks. I hung with the urban, pseudo-artsy-intellectual group who made fun of Greeks, who either ignored us or called us freaks, and who occasionally would sneak into one of their parties. They had great parties. But primarily, at Howard, I spent my years there in love with David, a graduate student. He was a lowly teaching assistant in the esteemed political science department there, searching, not sure if he wanted to become a full prof, as his old man was. Not sure he wanted to continue his membership in the class into which he was born; not sure what he wanted to do, be. I had my own parental issues, changing

my major from visual art to art history to theater arts before graduating, at my parents' insistence, with a liberal
arts degree. *You need something to fall back on.* The only
things that I loved were my art and photography classes.
That had been clear to me back then, but it was also clear
that Mama Leaver didn't think that was enough of an education, she was afraid for me to try to live an artist's life.
She believed it offered only heartbreak and that only people with real fortitude could make it. She didn't think I
had it. She didn't see me.

David was the first guy I'd ever been with who didn't try
to rip my clothes off as soon as we were alone. He took my
hand and would caress it as if examining every vein, liga-
ment and bone and talk slow about how he felt, how wonderful I was, how great we were together. On our dates
we'd go to magazine stores in Georgetown where we'd
spend hours looking at glossies from all over the world, on
all kinds of things from photography to textiles. We'd go to
out of the way art galleries. He always knew some tucked-
away joint—Ethiopian, Egyptian, Peruvian for dinner;
coffee shops, back when Starbucks was only a joint in
Seattle. We would linger. Talk politics—South Africa,
when Mandela was still in prison; Rhodesia—before it became Zimbabwe; black people—the reason we still ain't
free. He'd stroke his lush beard and tap his long pointer to
his temple. And every time he did it, I fell even deeper.

"What you willing to do to be free, Ina B. Wells?" he
would always ask.

It was his nickname for me. He'd say he loved my
name, Ina P. West, but couldn't resist the play on Ida B.

Wells, the antilynching freedom fighter. He never expected me to answer this, just liked to let me know what he expected of me—he wanted a thinking companion, not just someone who shared his bed. He loved to talk, almost as much as I loved to listen to him. So why then didn't we just stay together? Why didn't I move into his funky atelier with the view of a brick wall and a resident manager who had a thing for heroin, get a job downtown, maybe at the Corcoran—my favorite gallery where I had worked as an intern—and just kick it? Instead, he got caught up in a family fight because he had decided not to get his Ph.D. He went to work for the *Washington Post* as a clerk and went to law school at night, not because he wanted to be a lawyer, but as his silent rebellion. His father threatened to cut him off and I decided I had my own career indecision to tend to. I was trying to figure out what I wanted to be when I grew up. All I knew was that I didn't want to end up like my mother. David's family miasma was too much like mine and that scared me. I wanted someone who was free of drama—who could fill that requirement?

So I took the passive way out. I busied myself with my internship at the gallery, became vice president of the Campus Pals—if anybody knew Howard, I did, having been there for five and a half years—anything to occupy me so I didn't have to deal with David. I loved him but didn't want to. I figured it would just fizzle out, he'd get tired of me being unavailable and I wouldn't have to deal with anything. That didn't work. He just saw me whenever I "made" time. He continued to live alone inside his head, fighting with his parents. We'd get together, have hot, burning-down-the-funky-walls sex and I'd withdraw into my busy schedule. We even stopped going out to our favorite foreign restaurants. He said that I seemed tired of him and while that wasn't the case I just said yeah, that's it, too much for me to handle right now, so one day a couple weeks after graduation I turned over my sublet, packed up the Beetle and just went back home. I didn't even say good-bye.

After a couple months, when I started missing him, I called one drunken night only to hear a disaffected voice telling me he was glad to hear from me but had to go because he had "company," and he told me that he'd joined Vista and was going to Ghana to live for two years. He promised to call before he left the country. A week went by and then a month, then two and then four months. I called him again and his number had been disconnected. I'd lost him; at least that's what I told myself at the time. I decided he didn't want me anymore so I didn't want him. I let go of him. I let go of the idea of us.

THREE

J ay and I moved into our apricot-colored stucco Mediterranean-style center hall home with a circular drive five years into our marriage. I was pregnant with Marcus and Malcolm was four and Jay had decided we needed a backyard. It's the kind of house people slow down and point to as they drive by—beautiful curb appeal—sits back far, but not too, on a hill. It was our third home together, our first in the suburbs, and was supposed to be our final house, the one we were to be empty nesters in, the one we would have been in for thirty-five years, one of us still wanting to hold on long after we were too old and too small in number to enjoy. We'd fall apart each time the house was shown, sometimes in front of the younger, eager potential buyer. I would know which step Marcus tripped on and chipped his tooth, where Malcolm had carved his name, which hiding place was Ivy's favorite.

We're in the kind of real estate market where houses list for $600,000, sell for nine within two days, with twenty bids. Jay had been so busy over the last year and a half, we just didn't see him much, and on the few Sundays he wasn't working, he played golf. I understood how demanding a career it could be, especially in a market like this one. I gladly gave up my work when Jay's business picked up and he began hiring people, mostly attractive women with high-school age kids. I wanted to be at home more for the kids as they entered school. Selling was okay for a while, but when it's a buyer's market, the clients can really get on your nerves. Can you ask them to paint the master bedroom a different shade of yellow, or can they get rid of the pine on the basement walls? A seller's market is the time to be in real estate, when people will buy anything and make few or no demands. Of course watching nice sellers become money-grubbing ones is pretty disgusting, too.

I'd married Jay for the same reasons I couldn't have married David: he was tough and he was predictable. My mother's comment about Jay: "He's the kind of person who'll become successful but not get so biggety that you'd have to worry 'bout him becoming an Episcopalian and marryin' a white woman." That was as much an imprimatur as she'd ever give.

I met Jay officially after we'd graduated. I was at a club in downtown Newark—the Kenya Lounge. It was one of those places for the black "upwardly mobile." Professionals, the quasi and the non who worked for Prudential, Mutual Benefit, the telephone company and "the city" (of Newark); *a place to meet and greet after work*. The kind of place where you wear a suit, even if you don't wear one to work. It was all about business cards, Lancers rosé and Fonda Ray's *Over Like a Fat Rat*.

I was laughing with Michelle and Stacey, two friends from high school who I was reconnecting with since I was back at home. They had been my friends when I was in public school—I ricocheted between public and private my entire primary school life as my mother's political ideals clashed with her personal ones. When she was in her power-to-the-people phase, I was in public school and we stopped going to the *bourgeois beach* because the people there were *a negative influence with all their materialism*. Then when mom was into being purely an artist, I went to a progressive private school where the emphasis was not on reading and writing, but on developing the inner sense of each child. We went back to the *bourgeois beach* because *people are people*, she'd said, and she did a series of watercolors because the place was *incandescent*. Consequently, I had no tight group of friends from either place. I had my cousin Zackie and later David and Leelah. I was back in Pomona, working, trying to figure out what I was going to do with my life since graduating. I'd gotten together with Michelle and Stacey because Stacey had passed the bar. Michelle worked "for the city" and was selling Mary Kay on the side. I was working for legal services and trying to decide if I should go to art school or what. Jay walked in with a woman wearing a leopard print swing coat. Michelle and Stacey started calling her a hooker and Jay a pimp. He was shorter than the woman, who was otherwise wearing red from head to toe. He saw us laughing and he laughed, too. They recognized him from high school. After a while, when his date was on the dance floor, he came over to our table.

"So what y'all been up to?" Jay said, his smile seeming to take up his entire face. "Y'all work downtown?"

We nodded, more to the music than to his question.

He sat down next to Stacey, telling her he'd heard about her accomplishments and kissed her on the check.

Then he directed his attention to me.

"You really look familiar," he said to me.

"Oh brother," groaned Stacey.

"Boy, couldn't you do any little better than that," Michelle added.

I felt sorry for Jay, but he didn't seem to need my empathy.

"No really, you do. Did you go to Pomona High?" he pressed.

I looked at him, sizing him up, deciding he was cute even though short.

"Yeah, but not for long," I responded.

"I think I know you," he said.

"From Howard, stupid," Stacey said, nudging his side.

"Right, right. I knew I knew you. How you been?"

"Good," I said.

"So you're living here?"

"Yeah, for now. Tryin' to figure out my next move."

"So what are you into?" he asked.

"Well, I'm trying to decide whether I want to do the art school thing. Stacey here has been trying to talk me into law school."

"Yeah, girl, I say gone and bite the bullet. You don't have to practice but it's good training, especially when you can't figure out what else to do."

"That seems like a lotta work to do if you ain't tryin' to be Thurgood Marshall," Michelle said.

"True. I guess she could always sell Mary Kay," Stacey said.

Everyone laughed, even Michelle.

"Damn, that was cold," Jay said, leaning backward, pretending to dodge a hit. "Listen, I'm buyin', who wants a drink?" Jay said.

We all raised our hands and told him what we wanted. He mentally recorded our requests and went off to get them.

I leaned in over the low glass-and-chrome table between us.

"I don't remember him from high school," I said.

"I remember his obnoxious ass," Michelle said.

"Yeah, you remember him. He was like in student government, always president of something, walking around in a suit jacket and a briefcase," Stacey said.

"Nuh-uh," I said shaking my head. "I remember him from Howard, he was a Que and he was always with a different woman, who were all the same type."

"What's that?" Michelle and Stacey asked simultaneously.

"Tall with long hair."

"Plantation luggage," Stacey announced, like that was the ultimately condemning diagnosis.

"It must've been real bad at Howard," Michelle said.

"I can't say that. The crowd I hung with was definitely not into that. It seemed more like a southern thing, really."

"Looks like he's digging you right about now," Stacey said.

Michelle laughed and I told her to be quiet, although I was slightly intrigued by the idea.

"Nah, I don't think so. He's the kind of live Greek, die Greek, marry Greek who wouldn't be into the likes of me," I said.

"I have to say he's gotten cuter since high school," Michelle said.

Jay came back clutching three glasses together. We took them from his hands and thanked him.

He sat down next to me, and Michelle and Stacey bombarded him with questions.

"So Jay, what've you been up to?" Michelle asked.

Jay pushed his chest out a little more than usual and said he was selling real estate. "I also own a Dunkin' Donuts franchise."

I was looking into my drink, trying to stifle the urge to laugh, but saw Michelle and Stacy were impressed, probably doing math in their heads, coming away with the idea that Jay was making a good piece of change.

"So how lucrative is that?" Stacey asked.

"It's profitable. It's allowed me to buy up a few pieces of property—over behind Grant's. I fix 'em up to sell 'em."

"That's interesting," Stacey said.

"I'm also applying to grad school at NYU," Jay said.

"Really? In what," Stacey asked.

"It's in the business school but it's a real estate program for people who wanna do commercial and residential. Now I'm just doing residential, but I want to branch out."

Jay turned to me.

"So, what're you doing?"

I didn't want him to think that I was a total loser, especially sitting here celebrating Stacey becoming a lawyer and Michelle a step away from driving off with the pink Cadillac and him becoming the Donald Junior.

As he scooted his chair closer to mine, Michelle and Stacey took that as a clue to leave us alone and went in search for partners to hit the dance floor. I looked over to see his date was no longer dancing but at the bar, throwing her head back as some dude whispered in her ear. I guessed this wasn't a serious thing.

I sat there looking for Michelle and Stacey on the dance floor, knowing they'd be cutting up. They had a pudgy guy between them and they were freaking him. He held his head in the air, nose high like a dog's above water. The three of them looked as if they were having a ball.

"So Ina, where you living now?"

"I'm at home, for now, with the folks in Pomona."

"Oh yeah, I live in Pomona, too, not with my mom, though. I live at the Crestview. Maybe we can get together and have dinner or something?"

"Yeah, that would be nice."

"You busy tomorrow night?"

I laughed at the sight of Michelle and Stacey and said I was free.

So the next night I had my first date with Jay.

I got dressed thinking about where he'd pick for dinner. Would he want to go to one of the eclectic little bistros in town or one of the more adventurous we're-in-the-'burbs-but-we-want-you-to-feel-like-you're-in-Manhattan places or would we go into Manhattan? It was a little test, with me reading into his personality by which restaurant he'd choose. He showed up promptly at seven, dressed nicely casual, and said he wanted to take me to Spanish Tavern. A good compromise, I thought. It had a cute, unpretentious outdoor area that was romantic, but not overly so; the food was Portuguese and it was located "down neck" in Newark, not *the* city but a city. Okay.

"So you look different than you did at Howard," Jay said, practically the minute we sat down.

"It's the hair."

"Right, right. You had short hair in school."

"Mmm-hmm."

"It looks nice like that . . . I mean, not that it didn't before."

"Yeah, it's just in transition, like me, I guess."

I finished my glass of sangria and Jay poured more from the pitcher.

"You used to hang out with a guy, that guy who was a TA?"

"Yeah, David."

"You two seemed tight. You were always together. You still see him?"

"Oh, no. We broke up a while ago, after college, just grew apart, just life, I guess."

"Yeah, I hear that. So what is it that you want, Ina?"

Jay looked at me intensely, his eyes bearing into mine, causing me to feel off balance for the first time in the evening.

I adjusted myself in my seat.

"I guess I want what most people want, a family, a home, good friends."

These were just words. I had no idea.

"What about your work? Weren't you into photography or something? You were at the *Hilltop.*"

I smiled at the memory of the *Hilltop,* our college newspaper. I worked on the paper my entire time at Howard, practically living in the rundown row house on Bryant Street. I started as an occasional contributor, my best friend Leelah dropping off my pictures of tulips in front of the A building or Donald Byrd and the Blackbirds concerts at Crampton. I eventually became photo editor.

"I can't believe you remembered that."

"I noticed you at school. You always had that damn camera around your neck."

We both laughed at the memory.

"I think I even have some pictures of your frat, stepping on the yard or at a Step Show," I said.

"You do? I'd love to see them."

"I'll look through my stuff, see if I can find them."

At dinner Jay talked mostly about his career since leaving Howard, how much he loved college and how he still went back for homecoming any chance he got. I hadn't been back since graduation, but I didn't tell him that.

"So what about your photography? You plan to pursue it?"

"Eh, it's too iffy, you have to know people, you have to apprentice and you don't make any money. I just haven't kept going with it. You know, it's more like a hobby."

Jay was a see-it, do-it kind of person. I could feel his disappointment, or was it disapproval, as I heard myself making excuses for not pursuing something I'd once been so passionate about.

A few weeks after our first date I quit my job at legal services, ruled out art school and contacted my old boss at the Corcoran Gallery, who helped me get a job as a photographer's assistant in New York. A more apt description would be photographer's slave, but I loved the job, until something happened that changed me, killed all thoughts of a bohemian life, but I didn't know that then.

FOUR

M ommy had encouraged my artistic pursuits when
I was a child. The only time she shuttled me
around was for piano, dance and art lessons.
*Being an artist, a musician, a writer, is the best thing in the
world to be. To create something out of air, it's magical,
Ina.* She'd talk like this to me all during my childhood,
showing me her favorite artists' work, explaining brush
strokes and lighting. She was like a different person during these talks, like she could've been talking to anyone
or no one. She was inside her head, explaining her world,
her passion. But when I announced that I was an artist
and wanted to major in fine art photography in college,
she told me she wouldn't pay a dime for that. She didn't
want me to be miserable trying to be an artist and be a
normal person as she unsuccessfully had. *You can't strad-
dle, Ina. You'll make yourself crazy and you can't be an*

artist here, this country doesn't appreciate artists, you'll have to live somewhere else and I just don't think you're willing to do that. The only people who make it have fortitude like nails and I don't think you have that. Translation: If she couldn't do it, I couldn't.

Mama began her disconnect from reality around the time I was in college, around the time she retired from her teaching job. At first I didn't notice. She'd always been different, starting conversations at a midpoint, talking to herself, being absentminded in the extreme. She'd come home from work, pull the car into the driveway, get out of the car and leave the door open with the engine running. She'd put milk in the cupboard; forget to eat for days at a time. But Daddy was always there, kind of acting as her left brain.

She had become a closet painter after the time she had some of her stuff on display for sale at my private elementary school for a fund-raiser. She overheard some of the other mothers talking. "Who does she think she is? Matisse she is not," and she never let civilians see her work again. *They don't understand, baby,* my grandmother, a self-taught piano player, would tell my mother. Although she listened to her mother more than anyone else, nothing anyone said could convince her to show her work ever again. My grandmother played Chopin at home and gospel at church. I had piano lessons, but never wanted to practice. I couldn't imagine that I could ever get my fingers to do as Grandma's did. She would even slip me a dollar to practice and even then it was half-assed. I never liked

doing the same thing over and over and that's what practice meant, doing your scales over and over.

When I sat in my parents' kitchen one day after Jay had
left us, talking to my lucid mom while my dad played with
the kids in the basement, I listened as she smoked one
Marlboro after another.

"I went to the nice colored college in North Carolina
that your grandmother picked out, married your daddy—
again, someone she picked out—and had you. I knew you
were going to turn out exactly as you have and I'm sorry
baby, there was nothing I could've done to prevent it. You
came into all this bullshit, wearing all my stuff inside you,
all my shit. It's a crazy thing. I married a man who couldn't
kill a fly and you married one who . . ." she took a drag from
her cigarette and pursed her lips.

"Who wouldn't hurt a fly?" I added.

"I don't know. What can I tell you? Honor yourself. Be
you, be in this . . . shit . . . I sure as hell don't know how to
do it," Mama said. She had never seemed vulnerable to
me. I guess mothers rarely do, but now as she sat with me
over coffee and cigarettes, we were both beaten down from
trying to live a life that someone else had designed.

I was an only child, as was Zackie, who was a year older.
In some ways we were siblings, I used to wish we were,
but when his father used to beat him until his back was
red with stripes and some of them were opened, whitish
corpuscles exposed, I was glad we weren't. I'd cried for

him. I was the designated crier. I am easily touched by things and when I was younger I grew to be embarrassed by my tears and couldn't figure out why other people didn't cry as much as I did. Now I wonder the same thing, only I'm not embarrassed for me anymore. Now I feel sadness for the ones who are so hardened, untouched by anything.

So he was different. Everybody knew what Zackie was and everyone simply accepted him. In my uncle's mind, it was unacceptable.

It's the day of Zackie's birthday. I'm the first one at his party and his mother, my mother's sister, opens the door and the 45 "Love Makes a Woman" is playing on the hi-fi. It's the anthem this summer of '68. I'm dressed in a yellow-and-white polka-dot empire-waist party dress, white knee socks, black patent leathers with a small heel. Aunt Juneann, Zackie's mother, goes on about how pretty I look. . . . *When the fire, ah—it was burnin', yes it was . . .* , then she ushers me into her bedroom, sits me before the mirror attached to the dresser and starts to brush my hair. She squeezes my cheeks with one of her hands and says, "Humph, that face, I could just eat it up." She'd done that to me for as long as I can remember. I just figured it was the way she was, although I never saw her do that to Zackie. Zackie walks into the room, and says, "Mother, she ain't no doll, doll face." And everyone laughs. *I had someone, yes I did, call me honey and it's lo-ov-ve . . .* I was the only kid who came. The two sisters from down the street who were from down south but spent the summers in our neighborhood with their grandmother and Darren, the only boy in the neighborhood who didn't call Zackie names, were the birthday party regulars, but they didn't show up.

There were the usual adults there, my parents, our other aunt, Rayleen—who looked like a robust six-foot-tall Lena Horne; her new boyfriend; our sister-cousin Paris, who is eighteen and Aunt Rayleen's daughter but was raised by Aunt Juneann; Zackie's dad, Uncle Ben and his two brothers.

They all drink Schaefer and pretend not to notice that no kids have shown up and continue to have the same high-octave conversation that they always end up having. Mama, the only one in her family who went to college, the baby of the family, was the designated weird one.

"Leaver, what you doin' wit' that head now?" Aunt Juneann would say, starting in on Mama's hairstyle. Aunt Rayleen would add, "And how come you never try and get the damn paint off your hands, what's that about?" Depending on the day Mom would either ignore them or change the subject. She never told them to shut up or challenged what they said. She always felt like she couldn't, like she owed them for working to help send her to college. Aunt Rayleen owed Aunt Juneann, too, for taking in Paris and raising her as her own when Aunt Rayleen was too young and too disinterested to do it herself. Zackie just sat at the kitchen table, singing all the words, grunts and background vocals to "Love Makes a Woman," playing it over and over again. Zackie's mom, Aunt Juneann, fed us potato salad, fried chicken, green salad (iceberg lettuce and tomatoes) and dinner rolls. She never made kid food

like hot dogs and hamburgers. Zackie said that was because the party was as much for the adults as it was for his
birthday. He said this brutal truth the way he said most
things, flippantly, like nothing really mattered, but I knew
that it did because I was also his best friend.

"So who'd you invite this time?" I asked when we left
the adults in the kitchen and went out to the back porch.

"The same fucks I always do. I guess they all have decided it was time to cut the fag loose."

It was the first time I'd heard him refer to himself the
way everyone else in the neighborhood had for years.

"Why are you saying that?" I asked, even though I
knew the answer.

"Oh, it's true. I am what I am. You wanna play jacks?"

In the summer months, when both of our birthdays were,
we'd see each other every day, all day, moving from my
yard to the shed in his backyard that we used as our club-
house—we were a two-person membership. During the
winter we allowed a few others into our world, but they
never really got the jokes or understood Pig Latin. We'd
play kick ball and one two three red light and jump double Dutch and French. Zackie could jump better than
anyone. He'd jump in, his hands flayed like he was drying
his nails, feet operating the complicated patter as if they'd
been born to do just what they were doing. He'd jump a
circle on one foot, hold one foot up, tricks no one else
could do, and never get caught in the rope. While he was
doing all this jumping, he was the only boy. The rest of the

boys in the neighborhood were in the playground or in the street playing basketball or throwing a football or maybe playing a pickup softball game. Darren played with the boys, but we knew he was really close to us and would hang with us when the other boys weren't around. When they were they called Zackie names, sissy, fag and sissy fag. It got to be like a chant we could count on. In the beginning Zackie would respond usually with some retort so fierce everyone in earshot would start barking and yelling, "Wolf, wolf ticket, wolf ticket." And Zackie would proudly turn his attention back to what he was doing. Zackie would grow so tired of it he wouldn't even seem to let it in. But I knew better. I saw Zackie's shell grow. It didn't happen overnight. It was slow, at first, like ivy. A patch grew when he saw his mother squeezing my cheeks and pretended that it didn't bother him; another section was put on when Darren and the other kids didn't show up at his party; another piece when his father, the former high school jock, wouldn't take him to the plant picnic on father-son day. Aunt Juneann didn't keep secret her desire for a daughter and Zackie interpreted all her attention toward me as a rejection of him.

Zackie was big for his age and cocky enough to be able to convince Mr. Jackson, who owned the liquor store around the corner, that he was buying beer for his mother. Everybody knew Juneann loved her Schaefers so Mr. Jackson would just sell it to Zackie. He'd bring them back to Darren's house and we'd shake the cans and pop them so fizz would go all over. That was the excitement for us. Darren and I had no interest in drinking the beer, but Zackie would. He'd start out with one can and say he was "high" and began saying, "Come here, baby, give mama a kiss" to me. The likeness of the sound of Juneann's voice was remarkable. The facial expression, the voice, everything was his mother.

By the time we got to high school, Zackie was crossdressing. Twenty-five years before RuPaul, Zackie was dressing like a girl—some days more intensely than others. Sometimes he'd come to high school with his face fully made up, wearing a large Afro wig (he had different ones, both red and dark brown), sometimes he'd wear his own boy-short hair and a little eye makeup. He hung with a group of guys who tied their shirts at the waist, wore bandannas, tight jeans and sandals. He wouldn't even say hello to me when he was with his other dress-up friends, but most nights I'd be in my room and I'd hear the clack on the window, the pebble he'd throw, and I'd come downstairs and sit on the porch or in the hallway in my nightgown. "You know I can't stand living here," he said, trying to light one of his stolen Benson & Hedges.

"So who does?"

I sat there, digging my teeth into my cuticles. It was my brief stint in public school, when he and I went to the same high school. I felt the same outsiderness but I could blend in. Zackie couldn't, wouldn't.

He looked at me, this time with his Bette Davis eyes feeling sorry for me.

"I know what you're going through. This high school shit is a bitch, okay, trying to fit in and all, but darling, I'm telling you it ain't even worth trying, 'cause you and I don't. We don't fit in them little-ass boxes they have . . . ."

Sometimes Zackie talked over my head. Like when he used to go around saying he was paper brown tan all the time. I had no idea what he was talking about until I was grown. I listened carefully because I knew it would become clear if I just shut up.

"Cheerleader, sorority girl, football player, chess geek, honor roll, kiss-ass, those are your choices, darling, and guess what . . . neither one of us is going in any of those."

I stopped digging my cuticles and was now retying the tie of my nightgown. What he was saying was making my stomach hurt and I wanted him to stop, but I was also intrigued that he could plug right into what I was feeling. I wanted to hear who he thought I was 'cause I certainly didn't know. I looked at him, avoiding his amber eyes, 'cause I didn't want him to look into mine. His smooth skin without any makeup, his real hair close cut and tightly coiled, not big loose curls like his Afro wig. His mother knew he dressed up but wouldn't let him do it in front of his father, so at home he looked like a boy.

"You could fit in if you wanted to, I guess," he said sadly, "but not I. I simply don't have a choice."

"What are you talking about?" I finally said.

"I'm talking about *moi*, darling. I'm a fag and you, darling, you are a fag hag. You are fabulous, but not in any way that you understand. You're different and you're going to have a hard time until you accept that. I mean, look at your mother. Most people are boring and limited and want to be."

Boring I got, but limited? What the hell was he talking about?

"Just take this as a warning. Know that there's always a price for not being yourself."

He was scaring me.

"I gotta go anyway, gotta get my stuff."

His stuff meant his drag clothes. More and more he was taking the bus into Manhattan just to hang out with his friends and people who dressed like him. At night, dressed as a girl, he and Pebbles and other kids—they'd call themselves that—would hang out in Greenwich Village. Some dressed up, others didn't: none of them fitting into anybody's box. Zackie dropped out of high school the beginning of his junior year. It wasn't the work, he was always smart, could do the newspaper crossword puzzle when most kids were still learning to read, he was doing algebra in the fourth grade without breaking a sweat and the rest of us were just getting long division. He just couldn't stand the pressure to conform, of not being able to be who he was 24/7.

When I transferred to private school, I didn't see Zackie much. It was scary being without the person I could tell everything to. I would walk to the school bus alone, nod at a few people in the halls when I changed classes, but I felt weightless and insignificant. A boy named Michael who was popular and on the football team decided, I didn't know why, that he liked me. He started walking me to my bus. He was there on an athletic scholarship and seemed like a nice enough boy so we started going out. I didn't yet know the politics of the new school. I didn't know athletes were always at the top of the chain. I didn't know girls would be jealous that he was my boyfriend or that they would befriend me to get closer to him. I was wrapped up in the drive to fit in and if I needed to be a cheerleader to fit into the popular-girlfriend-of-the-football-player box, that's what I would do. Doing everything Zackie tried to warn me against. Since he'd dumped me, why would I believe anything he'd said? I hung out with girls who seemed to have a script of what life was and I happily played along. At least there was a script. At fifteen, sixteen one needs something to hold onto, a box to be in, otherwise life is way too scary.

CHAPTER FIVE

I t's my fall decorating time. I'm on the lawn putting up the bales of hay, scarecrow, pumpkins, cornucopia and my favorite, the witch on her broom who smashes into the tree. I like to do Halloween and Thanksgiving all together—especially now. I just want to get through these things. It's a hot mid-October and I'm wearing a light sweater over my nightgown, which is stuffed into my jeans, the baby monitor clipped to my back pocket. I've stopped bothering with dressing and showering has taken a backseat, as well. I think that I'm functioning just fine, all things considered. Jay sends checks regularly and pays the bills just like he did before, but otherwise there's been no contact. I think he's just too ashamed to face me, to talk to me. I would be. I'm on the lawn noticing, again, how pretty our neighborhood is— nannies and moms stroll by with their little companions, Volvo wagons and assorted SUVs and mini-vans are dropping off, I hear doors slam, kids' laughter, yelling to one another or a thank-you to Mrs. So-and-so. I suddenly feel strange, as if something has shaken loose inside me. I feel my insides getting mashed together and my face hot. For a second I thought it was some kind of fever flush, then my head began pounding and I felt water flooding my mouth; vomit emitted out of me like the slime machine Malcolm once got for Christmas. The force of it practically knocked me to the ground and then the tears started. I'd cried since Jay left—burning mad tears after seeing him in the paper with his new girlfriend; I cried into the kitchen sink, my back to the boys as they pressed me about their father's whereabouts and when he'd be coming back to live with us, but real, from the gut, what's-happening-how-could-he-do-this-kind-of-thing crying just hadn't happened. Until now, in the orange glow of this anomalous prewinter afternoon, out in the open for everyone who cared to look. I couldn't stop myself. I stayed on my knees, on the lawn, spit-up smell in my nostrils and I just cried, cried like Ivy does when we can't find her passie, that helpless, I'm-miserable, I-can't-take-it-anymore cry. I cried till my headache went away and came back again. I howled like a trapped dog. I didn't care if Paige or any other neighbor heard me. I cried until the dampness from my irrigated lawn that crept under my jeans made my knees feel stiff, and my hands were rough from handling straw. I went inside the house rubbing my hands, feeling like if I didn't get in the car and get away from here I'd pull off my skin and that of the next person I saw. I stood in my kitchen and tried to do what I've always done: organize the rest of my day, the week, mentally checking off kid activities and carpool responsibilities. I tried to remember who was doing to-day's pickup and I couldn't remember what day it was. My mind had gone blank, shut down like a computer during a power surge. Nothing was there and I couldn't recall it with all my effort. I sat down and tried to calm myself by breathing deeply. All I wanted to do was get out of my world, which used to feel like a hermetically sealed box—boring but secure. The box had been punctured, upturned, and I'd been crushed inside. The life I'd chosen, I thought at the time, so carefully tailored to fit, no longer does. My husband is gone and is spending all his time with her, buying nice presents for her, rubbing lotion on her feet. I called my dad and told him that I needed to get away for a while, a few days maybe even weeks. The kids hated being at my parents' house because my mother's behavior was so erratic. It scared them. I couldn't think about that now. I was crying but trying in vain to keep him from hearing me.

"Ina, are you okay, baby?"

I couldn't stop sniffling.

"No," I said, sounding like I was six and had just fallen off my new two-wheeler.

"I'm comin' over there."

"No, Daddy. I'm leaving. Ivy'll be at Paige's. Just pick up the boys and get Ivy later . . ."

"Okay. Okay. You take your phone with you. I'll check on you in about an hour, okay?"

"Okay."

I just wanted to get off the phone and get outta the house.

I went into Ivy's room where she was taking a nap and

took her right to Paige's. I didn't even go through all the motions of reminding her of their schedules. By now she knew them as well as I did and I couldn't think of half the shit anyway. None of it seemed very important right about now.

"My dad'll pick her up later. He's getting the boys."

"Ina, I know this has to be hell," Paige said, in her straightforward Indiana-bred way. "You can always count on me."

I was so grateful that she never made me feel like I had to tell her all about it. She wasn't one for gossip over coffee, even though she knew everybody's business. People told her things because they knew she was discreet. She could intuit when someone needed to talk, and when, like now, couldn't.

I somehow got back to my house, went upstairs and threw a few pairs of underwear, nightgowns, jeans and sweaters into a leather duffel. I even threw in my favorite jersey dress. I didn't know where I was going; I just knew I had to get away from here. As I packed some gifts from Jay, I now see they were guilt-ridden pacifiers: the bulging emerald ring suspended by pavé diamonds; a citron-colored cashmere shawl; a strand of South Sea pearls. I'd wear the stuff when I was having lunch with my PTA cohorts. They'd *oh* and *ah* and tell me how lucky I was, how much Jay loved me. I needed to hear that because I didn't trust what I knew: that these presents were more about him than me. He needed for people to see how much money he had. He needed to have a wife who would wear a $20,000 necklace to the supermarket.

I headed to the highway, somewhere away from New York, away from my invisibility, away from my counterfeit life. I drove to the New Jersey Turnpike; past Ikea, past signs for Great Adventure, past exits for Philadelphia. I didn't stop until I got to a rest stop directly in front of the Delaware Memorial Bridge. I got out. It was getting late. Malcolm would be getting panicky and Dad would have to talk him through it and he'd do the same for Marcus.

I rinsed my face with cold water and tried to dry it with one of those brown paper towels; paper pulp stuck to my face and I looked like I had some form of chicken pox. I rinsed again and let my skin air dry. I got back in the SUV, and continued south on 95. Two hours later I pulled into a gas station on New York Avenue and asked the Arab attendant if he had a telephone. I smiled sweetly as I explained that I'd left my phone at home. He softened and pointed inside, to his office, his private phone. I called Information. He had a common name, it wouldn't be easy. I was prepared to call all twenty numbers under that name. At the ninth, I got him. The noise from the TV in the background was loud. He answered curtly, something like "What up?" or "Speak," or something rude. I said his name with a question mark. He paused and stammered and muted the TV that had been blasting in the background.

"Where are you?" he said urgently.

"I'm here."

He let out a blast of air, as if he'd been holding his breath for all these years, the ones that stood between us, the ones that we had sleepwalked through. I'll be right there, he told me. I hung up the phone and held onto the receiver, relieved and scared. I got back into my SUV, punched the buttons on the radio, moving from one black station to another—there were many in Chocolate City; the Quiet Storm with Regina Belle belting out "Come to Me"; the Commodores singing about the sister with the "brick house" body on one of the new oldies stations; Puffy and crew remixing it on the number one black Top 40 station; Jay-Z on the all-rap station. Finally I turned it off, looked at the clock knowing that Ivy would've been fussy and hungry, hoping Dad had let Paige and Ingracia keep her. They would manage to fix something that Ivy would smack her lips for in hearty approval.

When I heard the aggressive-sounding engine, I just knew the slightly beat-up, faded blue vintage BMW was his. I knew it was David's car before it lurched into the gas station—it was just the right statement of genteel poverty he needed to make, a pose he was most comfortable with, that he'd vehemently worn in this headquarters of status symbols. He'd come right away, but the wait had felt like years as I sat in my ultrastatus-conferring vehicle. Suddenly, what the white Range Rover said about the life I'd chosen embarrassed me. I knew David tallied it all up and disapproved.

I followed his car to an out of the way café in Adams Morgan. Once we'd parked in a lot, we awkwardly greeted each other with a butt-away hug and dry kiss. Inside the restaurant, I followed him and the hostess—who said she recognized him from his picture on his column—to a private table. After two glasses of wine and some talk about who was doing what from school, he reached across the table and put his hand over mine. We were looking deeply at each other before I had to turn away from the heat of his stare. It had always been powerful. We kept the conversation light, but I'm sure my presence was saying everything I wouldn't, or more accurately couldn't, say. His job was going well. He'd been promoted several times before getting his own weekly column. His bosses were pressing him to go into management, become an editor, but he wasn't interested. He was seeing several women, none of them important enough to talk about, nothing like . . . well, you know, he said before trailing off.

"So where you staying?" he asked as he neatly folded the receipt for our drinks, my salad and mushroom puffs and slipped it into his wallet.

I had expected to stay with him, but figured I could always hook up with Leelah.

"I don't want to intrude on your life," I blurted without anything resembling finesse. "I think Leelah lives in Adams Morgan."

"She does, but you can stay with me. It's no big deal. I got a house now, plenty of space."

He smiled at me as we both remembered the wee walkup on U Street that he used to call home. We had made love all over the cracked plaster walls, the rickety aluminum kitchen table and the futon that we'd pull onto the fire escape when it got too hot to sleep inside. Being together, we could reminisce about who we were back then. I was a broke Howard student rich in love and excited about learning, about life, about finding myself; and he was a lowly teaching assistant in the esteemed political science department there, a graduate student, searching for the big answers, too.

"Thanks," I said, filled with gratitude for the second time today.

Chapter Six

I jumped, the way you do when you feel yourself falling inside a dream and jerk to stop yourself. Opening my eyes to see the unfamiliar deep cranberry walls that seemed to be falling in on me caused my heart to race. I looked over and recognized my clothes thrown over a dark purple velvet armchair. I'd slept in his pajamas. We drank a bottle of port, but not so much that I couldn't recall last night. I knew nothing had happened and that I had slept alone. I couldn't remember the last time I woke up in a strange bed, alone. For thirteen years I'd been part of something—a couple, a family bed. There was no sleeping alone, one or two, sometimes they all piled into our bed; there were no vacations on my own, not even an overnight with a girlfriend. I used to be a loner, loved my solitude. How did I let go of all of that?

David hadn't even tried anything last night. He could probably tell that my state was more than a little fragile. I heard him moving around downstairs and felt happiness, then weirdness in my bones. I knew I'd have to at least call home to tell Daddy and Paige where I was. They'd be reassuring, but I would feel irresponsible like I was also abandoning my children. I fingered the pearl studs I always wore, Grandma Caledonia's, and pushed against my instinct to worry about my kids, particularly Marcus, who was having the hardest time since the breakup. I reassured myself that he was fine. Grandma would've approved of my little escape. "Who said women bonded with their babies like some gorilla in the damn jungle?" Grandma would pronounce after several bourbons at a family dinner. I had mixed feelings about the whole motherhood thing. I hadn't planned to become a mother when I did, but when I first saw Malcolm, held him, kissed his little damp head, I finally understood what all of it was about. But at that moment at David's I was happy that I didn't have to nurse boo-boos and sing lullabies and rub A and D onto the baby's soft bottom, fix breakfast, pack lunches, make Marcus brush his teeth. I wanted my freedom, to feel my self, my old self who used to be a student and a thinker and a doer. I didn't understand how much a child sucks from you. It wasn't that I wanted to dress up in Dolce & Gabbana and hang out at nightclubs, but I wanted my mind, my thoughts, some of my original self back. The one who had had ambition and dreams and loved going to foreign films in the middle of the day. I didn't want to have every single second accounted for, having to pick up, feed, bathe and read to someone else, every single day and night. The monotony of doing that on top of PTA, soccer, violin lessons, Baby and Me classes was literally killing me and no one, no one told me it would be like this, except maybe that was what Mama, with her mixed communication, had been about: raising me to be a nice traditional woman—forget about being an artist—her disappearances, depressions because she was one. Her actions told me that the road is too hard, have a safe life. She wanted to protect me. Of course you do, you love your children, but your own desires don't just vanish, maybe they're supposed to, but that didn't happen to me and it certainly didn't happen to Mama. All people tell you is how you love the baby so much and that that's all you'll want to do. It's only partially true—you love them totally but you still want to do other things that don't involve them. In my mother's group I felt like the worst kind of fraud because as much as they complained about missing their professions, they all seemed content to just be with their babies all day long. I wasn't. There were days when Malcolm and Marcus were little, and Jay would be gone fifteen hours a day, when I thought if someone didn't come over so that I could have an hour to myself, I'd pull my eyeballs out. I do love my children more than anything, but why should I feel like a felon for wanting to also have some of my life for me?

I pulled on my jeans and a turtleneck, took a quick look into what was clearly his bedroom and ducked into the bathroom to wash my face and brush my teeth with toothpaste on my finger.

"Morning. You sleep good?" he said, looking over his reading glasses.

I sighed and shook my head yes. When did he start wearing glasses, I wondered?

"I made some coffee and there's Danish, or cereal if you want."

He'd set out mugs and cream, sugar dish, all matching blue ceramic trimmed in brown. His neatly decorated house seemed to run as well as mine. I didn't bother sharing my observation.

I poured coffee and slid in a corner nook, across from him at the table, as naturally as if we'd been doing this for years. He was intently reading the national section. I watched him, listened to his hardly audible grunts, released whenever he came across something especially abhorrent.

"So," he turned to me when he was finished, folding the paper and putting it on top of the rest, removing his glasses.

"So," I said, looking into his eyes.

"Do you feel like telling me what's going on?"

I lifted the mug to my lips and sipped, bracing myself for what I knew I had to say.

"I didn't know where else to go. I don't know what's going on . . ."

Mmm was all he said.

He was never one to hold back, but he did.

"I don't know. I couldn't breathe. I had some kind of an attack and had to just get away."

"So life with Mr. Perfect ain't so perfect?"

I took his sarcasm; let it hit me on the chin, thinking that somehow I deserved it.

"It's, um, a little more complicated than that," I said, reaching for the cream.

"For a while, whenever we talked you were fine, at least that's what you said."

"I was fine, for a while."

"So what happened?"

"Jay left."

David was silent and the look on his face told me he really was at a loss for something to say.

"Don't look at me like that," I said.

He looked down again, knowing that we knew each other too well to bullshit. *Don't pity me* is what I meant and he understood exactly.

"Well, how are things? Are you okay? The kids . . ."

"I'm okay, but I had to get out of there, out of my house, my town, the damn state . . ."

"I can understand that, sure. What can I do?"

"Nothing, just what you've done. Be my friend, remind me of who I was."

I'd heard through our network of college friends that David had been disappointed in me for marrying Jay, whom he thought shallow, a man without any convictions. He hated fraternity guys on principle.

"People who join groups are sheep, Ina," he'd rant whenever we passed a group of Greeks stepping on the Yard. I'd always want to stop and watch, even shoot them.

He would refuse and lecture me. I secretly thought they were sexy and did take their pictures whenever I was alone.

"So what are you gonna do now?"

"I have no idea."

"Maybe this is just a midlife crisis," he said, without conviction.

I finished my coffee and got up to put it in the sink. I leaned on the blue tiled island and looked at him. His brow was knitted, as it often was.

"I lost myself somewhere. . . ." My voice cracked and tears flooded my eyes.

David got up from the table and took me in an embrace that was pure. He held me and let me sob, just listening to me cry, comforting me like you do a baby when there's nothing to be done other than soothe.

CHAPTER SEVEN

"You never did answer my question," I said as we drove along the Potomac.

The car, even one with this belligerent drone, was always a good place to talk to David.

I was referring to one of his many letters; letters that he'd write me occasionally. After Malcolm was born, I'd heard David was back in the States. I reached out to him, sent him an announcement, he wrote me back a letter I still have. I countered with a postpartum call that probably scared him. His letters were musings of a mad black man; a brilliant writer who I thought was wasting his talent as a reporter. Yeah, it's a good paper, a big respected one, but was still a newspaper and I thought he should've been writing novels, essays, something more. For months I would live for one of his letters, then I'd carry it around in

Malcolm's diaper bag, until milk or juice would get to them and the ink would bleed.

"Could you love inside parameters?"

David smiled at the memory.

"What do you think?"

"I think, probably not."

He turned the steering wheel hard to the right to park against a small embankment.

"Ina, I think that depends on who you're talking about loving. If you're talking about you, then yes. I could have loved within parameters."

I stupidly felt relieved, happy because of his useless answer.

"You never answered mine," he said.

He used to ask me life questions through musical references. One was, "Can you go from Aretha to Tupac to Al Jarreau to Ray Charles to Coltrane to Miles to LL to Hendrix to Stevie Nicks to Stevie Ray Vaughn to Stevie Wonder to Nina Simone to the Ohio Players to Joni Mitchell?"

"Yeah, the answer is yes."

He looked at me and raised an eyebrow.

"I can't believe you remembered that," David said.

"Why not? I remember everything, every conversation, every time we made love, what we ate together and what the weather was like when we had an argument. Everything."

Not many things surprised him, this had.

David was attractive, had a sharp mind and a deep empathy for the less fortunate. He was a rebel. He grew up among D.C.'s "best and brightest." His mother was the first female partner in one of the city's oldest law firms before chucking it to start a national organization for impoverished children. His father was a nationally regarded antiquities professor at Howard. David was the youngest of three boys and the only one his parents sent away to boarding school because he was too much for them to handle, staying out all night, drinking beer all day and generally going nowhere fast—except in stolen cars along Beach Drive in Rock Creek Park. Jay had been the opposite because he knew he didn't have any cushion, he couldn't fuck up. David was sent to Memphis, to Christian Brothers Prep, for his maternal grandmother to straighten him out, put some old-school sternness on him, something that his parents weren't capable of. Now that he'd landed on his feet, no one was prouder than his parents. Even though both his brothers also had achieved mightily, they didn't seem to have the compassion that David had or the drive to deal with the schizophrenia necessary to be black, successful and sane. They just checked out. One brother was an economist who married a German and lived in Paris, the other was a research scientist in Boston, married to a Vietnamese physician. For his parents, the prize always went to the one who'd traveled the most complicated route and David seemed to choose the rougher terrain.

I saw David's luminosity almost two decades ago, just as I did at this moment as he spread a blanket over the grassy knoll at the Jefferson Memorial. I remembered how much I loved to just hear him talk—about anything. One of his favorite topics—the black bourgeoisie and how pathetic they were, for all that potential being wasted on just emulating white folks, who're floundering like everybody else, and the deep psychic damage on the entire race because of slavery, showing up in everything from gangster identification to skin color and so-called "good" hair obsession. Plantation luggage. He could go on for hours and I could listen for that long, even though I'd heard it all before. It was often the subject of his columns and why he was loved or loathed in D.C. Nothing in between. He was celebrated and demonized equally by the masses and the city's haut monde.

I sat munching on a tuna sandwich looking at David, remembering the high I'd get from just listening to him, the readiness that was always inside me whenever we were together. I wanted him right now, but resisted the urge to pull him toward me by the collar and plunge my tongue into his mouth.

"What I remember was you and your expectations. They were so high, I was afraid. Who could live up to—"

"You were all I wanted, but then the whole thing with your dad and you not knowing what you wanted to do scared me. I needed you to be together, 'cause I wasn't. Now, looking back, I see that we were both dabblers in this romantic bohemian thing but neither of us had a clue about how to make a life," I said.

"Yeah and I still don't, but you, you . . ."

He looked out over the Potomac before turning to look at me.

"You figured it out . . ."

I closed my eyes at those words. I didn't want to hear his condemnation.

He turned his gaze back to the river.

"Look at where you ended up," he finally said.

I sat on the rough Mexican quilt and rubbed my forehead, trying to envision the young woman I was in D.C.—proudly going braless, wearing my hair natural and declaring myself a womanist, a free-thinking black person who was out to change society. Even I had to admit that that person seemed like a stranger to the person sitting on David's blanket. I looked at myself the way I know I appeared to him. My short curly Afro that he knew had been replaced by long, straightened hair parted down the middle, my wrist anchored by my gold watch with diamonds circling the face, a wedding band put together of diamond chunks big enough to be a skating rink for ants, all reminders of my acceptance of, my acquiescence, to David's rejected world.

"David, I just didn't know what I wanted. Didn't you know that?"

"Yeah, I knew that, but I also felt this pressure, that we had to be together in a certain way, in some context, and when you just up and left . . ."

I felt my head getting hot.

It was true at the time I believed that I could be a fringe-mixed person, have the traditional life with marriage, a house with a slate patio, but live out of the box. We'd travel and eat exotic food and know interesting people and . . .

"Yeah, I wanted us to get married at some point. I thought that we would. I thought we were good together, I thought you thought that, too," I admitted.

"And you left, so obviously you didn't really want any of that with me." He said it flatly, like, *Checkmate, sister, end of game and conversation. You left and that's the bottom line.*

David closed his eyes and rubbed his face with both hands.

I looked at his beautiful, smart face and felt my insides melt. The one thing that was the same was the way he moved me, affected me and thrilled me. It was a longing I'd often overheard my mother and aunts talk about, that there was always one who could get to you, beneath all your shit, your layers of self-protection that covered you like insulation and Sheetrock. When you caused a similar reaction in him, it was a force stronger than water or fire. But you didn't *marry* the man you felt this for; it never worked. It's like the idea of a used car without problems or an old house that's without rotten windows or a new one that has charm. You can't have both—at least that was what Ma and her sisters had believed. Aunt Rayleen was testimony. She had had an illegal abortion and bled to death because her man, her husband—her one and only love—had told her to. He didn't want to have children, had told her so when they first met. She'd had to live with giving up one child—her daughter, Paris, because she'd been born out of wedlock in a time when without the lock women were at risk—she didn't want to give up another one. In the end, when the embryo was too far along, Rayleen did what her husband demanded and paid for that decision with her life.

"You went to Africa and I couldn't tell you that I'd had a change of heart," I finally said to him.

"I felt like I didn't have a choice," he said, pleadingly.

"But why didn't you just talk to me?"

"I don't know, Ina. I've asked myself that more than you know."

I had told myself I wouldn't ask him why, because what difference did it make now. I wasn't still available to him, was I?

CHAPTER EIGHT

That night I found myself at a window table at Kincaid's with two of David's friends, each famous or semifamous. I'd wanted to invite Leelah, but David didn't think the mix would be right. She had been my closest college friend. The only person besides Zackie who I let see all my sides, not just pieces. There was a lot of that in college—segmenting selves to fit in certain crowds, pieces floating about like ribbons at a Maypole dance. Leelah just understood me and I her and I hated that my life with Jay pushed her out. She remained single long after I got married and I let him convince me that it was somehow disruptive for a married woman to have unmarried friends. So we slowly parted, talking only twice a year, on her birthday and mine and eventually those calls came a day or two after, as did the cards, and then not at all. But when I went to homecoming with Jay last year, back when we were still pretending to be a reasonably happy couple, Leelah and I finally reconnected.

I reluctantly agreed not to invite her and after meeting David's friends I had to agree that the mix wouldn't have been right. The walls of the restaurant were painted a kind of deep blue with streaks of lighter cloudlike strips running vertically. The kitchen was one of those open-air ones in the center and emitted lots of steam no other patrons seemed to notice. It was the power media joint of the moment where everyone had a regular table and one's status was easily judged by the type of table one had. David's was center close to the window, but not the prime window spot. Appropriate for the comer he was. His friend Todd, who was an advisor to the president and a commentator on a network affiliate, had a better table at which we all sat.

"So Ina, you and David were college sweethearts?" Todd began right after we'd ordered drinks.

"Damn, man, can't we have a drink before the inquisition begins?" David said, laughing.

"So what was Dave like in college?" asked Jennifer, an attractive Korean-American TV journalist. "Was he a knucklehead then?"

"You don't have to answer that," David said.

"Ah, but I want to," I said. I couldn't remember when I'd last had so much fun.

I didn't know if it was the alcohol or the company or feeling free again. I'd gone two days without having to sweep up Cheerios, unload the dishwasher, clean boo-boo diapers, carry, rock, deliver water at 3:00 A.M. I'd actually slept through consecutive nights without being summoned by a bad dream or hunger. The feeling was intoxicating, as were the memories of incredible sex with David. I told myself I wouldn't feel guilty, although after drinking three margaritas fast I felt something akin to guilt creeping around the edges, missing my children like an amputated limb.

"He was the most interesting, sexiest man I'd ever met," I'd answered his inquiring friends.

My answer was met with a brief silence, then whoops and high fives around the table.

If this was true, what was I doing married to someone else, I hoped they didn't ask that. I also hoped that they didn't know I was married with kids, but I knew David would have told them. It made for a better story and he'd go anywhere for a good story.

Initially they were gracious enough not to say anything about my status, but after we moved around the corner to a private cigar club, grace melted away.

"So Dave tells us that you've left your family for him," Todd said, cutting his Cristo.

I was stung and looked at David, who looked down into his brandy snifter.

"That's not quite accurate," David said. "Let's talk about somebody else's shit, shall we?"

"Well," Jennifer said, "my life is so boring that it would take about five minutes to give all the details."

"Hey, hey. Look at whom you're out with. You have a great life," Todd said.

"So what do you do, Ina, in—where is it—New York? New Jersey?" Todd asked.

"Yes. Well, let's see. I'm a mom; I send my kids to school, I pick them up. I take one to soccer and violin, the other to art and karate and I do baby exercise with my seven-month-old daughter. I shop, make dinner, belong to the PTA, go to book club meetings and go to dinner parties. That's what I do."

I'd obviously sounded hostile and probably a little useless 'cause suddenly the table got quiet.

Jennifer jumped in and asked if I had any pictures of my children. I liked her for that.

I pulled out a few that I'd managed to stuff into my tote bag before I'd left. Malcolm standing on the soccer field in his uniform and a ball tucked under his arm; half smile and curly uncombed hair, looking more like me than Jay. Marcus in a Spider-Man costume, smiling so hard it looked like his face might crack and Ivy in a pink puffy-sleeved dress with orange smocking, hands in her lap, plump like a pumpkin.

"My God, the baby looks exactly like you," Jennifer said, passing them on to Todd, who gave a cursory glance and nod.

"So has David's allure faded?" Todd asked.

"He still has it," I said, smiling at David, who looked uncomfortable and picked up his cigar and took a drag, puffing smoke out so that his face was almost covered.

"So maybe you guys'll pick up where you left off," Todd said, a little edge in his voice.

"Let me see the pictures," David said, willing to do anything to change the subject.

"Is this Malcolm?" David asked.

He subtly lifted his finger for the waiter.

"That's him."

Todd had clearly grown bored of the family pictures routine.

"Well, good people, I gotta go, gotta do my pundit thing in the early morn," Todd said.

"Oh yeah. I'm getting a ride with you, right?" Jennifer said, turning to me. "It was really nice meeting you, Ina. See ya later, Dave."

"Yeah, yeah, I'll see you later guys," David said, distracted by their abrupt departure.

David was biting at his upper lip, a habit he'd had for as long as I'd known him. He did it when he was angry or confused or during any number of uncomfortable emotional situations. Like so many things about him, it was another thing that made him so attractive. His ways pulled women to him, they were involuntary reflexes; he wasn't especially charming or even solicitous, he just had that thing, that unnamable thing, a scent that certain people just have. It was never about looks or status, although having those things certainly helps; it's just something you have to be born with and David was. The thing Warren Beatty had. David had broad shoulders and a powerful jaw-line that used to be covered by a beard so luscious I could spend the day just stroking it. It was thick and full and it shone, he had a high forehead that made him seem regal and lips that were just this side of pouty and as soft as any baby's. He had lashes and eyebrows people pay good money to emulate. He was the kind of man who appealed to all kinds of women regardless of race or class.

But for me, what made him most appealing was that he seemed genuinely not to know that he was fine. I learned it just wasn't something he seemed to value. Most men who look as good as David can grow to depend on it, they become lazy. They don't have to call 'cause they know someone will call them, they don't have to think of interesting dates 'cause the woman is just glad to be with him, sitting on a curb eating ice cream or whatever happens to be in the refrigerator. I wondered if David had become one of them. After we said good-bye to Todd and Jennifer, we sat at the café table, silent for a while.

"So Malcolm is how old?"

"Thirteen, and Marcus is nine. I know it's a shock."

"Where did the time go?"

"It must really feel that way when you don't have kids."

"Ah, yes. I remember so vividly after Malcolm was born and you called me."

"Yeah, you were having a party . . ."

"I don't have parties, there were people over for the game . . ."

"Whatever."

"Yeah, I remember you telling me the details of his birth and it totally blowing my high. I wanted to listen, be a supportive friend, but I'm thinking, Ina, I really don't wanna hear this . . ."

"You shoulda said something."

"No, I should've done what I did, listen."

We walked back to David's place. It was evening in fall and I wasn't dressed for the change.

"You cold? You want my jacket?"

I was, but didn't want it. "No, no, I'm okay. It feels good."

"You've changed," David said, as we started a faster pace.

"How?"

I was waiting for some brilliant insight, a comparison between my old and new character.

"You used to get cold in seventy-degree weather," David said, laughing at the memory.

"Yeah." I chuckled, disappointed, but not letting it show. I was cold, but wanted to feel it, be uncomfortable for a few minutes, sober myself up a little.

Now I was miles away from home, from my kids, in my old lover's house, wanting to be that girl I was, make love on his couch and be free. But I was not.

We got to his house and I concentrated on wiping my feet on the welcome mat as he put the key in the lock.

I looked around the living room where stools and masks from Ghana were artfully displayed, magazines sprawled on the leather couch and a glass coffee table had another stack of magazines and books neatly piled. His stereo equipment took up half a wall and CDs, cassettes and albums another. He liked all kinds of music: jazz, funk, Brazilian, reggae, all kinds of world music, classical, rock. It was the one thing I never understood about him. How could anybody have such broad musical taste? It felt like an inability to commit, to me, and I'd told him so on more than one occasion in our early life together.

"So what you wanna do? Wanna watch a movie? Listen to some tunes? Have sex?"

I laughed nervously because I truly didn't know what else to do. I wanted to talk, but I wanted him to want to. I thought he'd be dying to, but he wasn't. To him, it was like, *Okay you're back; let's just pick up where we left off seventeen years ago.*

"Just kidding," he said, holding up his hands, palms out.

"Let's watch a movie, but I need to make a phone call first."

NINE

Mom answered the phone, humming the theme song to *Jeopardy*.

"Ma, is that you?" I said, knowing it was, hoping to help her back to reality.

"Ina? Is that you, baby?"

"Yeah, Ma, it's me. Turn the TV down." It was too late for *Jeopardy*.

"The TV? Oh, okay, okay, hold on a minute."

She was gone for almost two minutes. I could picture her as she sat on the floral slipcovered sofa, her glasses on crooked, a housedress over corduroy pants. Looking dazed.

"Okay, I'm back. You comin' over?"

"No, Ma. I was just calling to see how the children were."

"Oh, they're fine, Ina. That Malcolm is a shy one, huh?"

Thankfully Dad picked up the extension.

"Hi, dear. Everything okay?" he said.

"Yeah, Dad. How're the kids?"

"Good. We were down in the basement playing pool before they went to bed. Paige came and got Ivy today and she's still there. Is it okay if she spends the night there?"

"Oh yeah, that's fine. So the boys are sleeping?"

"Yeah, mmm-hmm. Your mother doesn't do too well with the baby around."

"Yeah, I know."

"Leave me your number and we'll call you in the morning."

"Okay, but I'll call them before they leave for school."

"Okay. Well, we'll talk to you later."

Dad always talked in the phone louder and more concentrated than usual.

I called Paige and she was her usual glib self. While she reassured me that Ivy was fine and that I should take as much time as I needed to fix whatever needed fixing and I believed her, our relationship had gone past neighbors to friends but there was a partition, a wall created when she said something that I couldn't get past. Our relationship had changed and was now like the town we lived in—it looked great, but there was something underneath that wasn't quite right. Pomona was a city of contrasts, a lot like me. It embraced the notion of diversity long before that was a part of our national lexicon, but living it, like reality, was far more complex. There are *Town and Coun-*

try estates ten minutes away from rundown multifamilies. Some of the rich folks in multimillion-dollar homes send their kids to public schools—like Paige and Andy. There's always been a vibrant mix of middle- and working-class folks all together; the town has jazz musicians, poets, lawyers and teachers, postal workers and artists; art galleries and good schools.

When Jay and I moved back, I thought we'd found it: that impossible place—good schools for the kids, a stimulating atmosphere for adults with bookstores and coffeehouses, a museum and a movie theater that showed foreign films, pretty parks and lots of restaurants. But it was far from Shangri-la.

My discontent with the town began with the beads in the trees. I decided to put Mardi Gras beads in my trees. My neighbors at first said "charming," although later, through Paige, I heard "weird." When a black person does something like that it's always more loaded than it should be. The "there goes the neighborhood" feeling was palpable. Someone even remarked, "Her husband's in real estate, for God's sakes, she should know better." I had thought Pomona was better. Jay chalked my behavior up to being postpartum; that was when he began leaving presents around the house. He would never just say to me, "Is there something wrong.?" Each time I opened one, I wished they could've done what he'd intended . . . appease, please, distract, stop me from making a spectacle of myself, our house and by extension him. But I wouldn't be appeased or pleased or distracted or stop what I was doing. There was a time in my life that I'd lived by my artist's sensibilities and the beads in the trees were my attempt to say something, to scream, to make a statement, to call for help.

I was once free and curious and loved nothing more than gathering around a table with a bottle of wine, discussing books and films and art. I used to go to the movies in the middle of the day and feel so satisfied, like I had when I worked at the Corcoran in D.C., talking to photographers about their work for our newsletter. I felt fulfilled. Then it just all changed and I opted for an easy way, for a life in the box. There are good things about being in a box . . . it's secure, you know where you are at all times. Of course, it's also suffocation but I didn't know that when I chose it. Edit the artist out and get your hair done. It's so much easier and then you think we're all wearing bunny ears and the group nods back yes we are, and isn't it great and what about the box and they say yeah, we're all in a box but isn't it nice and clean and safe. There's so much stuff waiting to attack you and so you just stay in the box because it's easier to wear the clothes your mother laid out for you.

Around the same time as the beads in the trees, there had been two car thefts in our neighborhood—in broad daylight. One that had happened in the early morning hours, the victim had even seen the gang of teenagers through his window when he'd gotten up to go to the bathroom. They were white kids so the victim just thought they were his neighbor's son and his friends. So we thought the band of thieves were white kids who could move about the neighborhood unnoticed. Then they were caught. So when

Paige's car was stolen and she came over to tell me to be careful, her adrenaline still pumping from having seen them through her kitchen window, whisking away in her luxury SUV in broad daylight.

I asked the question all guilt-ridden privileged black folks ask: Were they black?

"Of course," she blurted, her eyes widening. I didn't know if she was clueless about her gaffe or if she didn't care. I knew she believed that there were niggas—the people who stole her car—and there are black people, me. Niggas throw garbage out of their windows rather than walk down and place it in garbage cans. Niggas cuss the bus driver out for asking them to turn down the music, put the cigarette out, fill in the blank. Niggas come in all colors, but I couldn't feel the same about her after that. At the time I didn't know why.

Ten

We begin to wrestle, I was on the top . . . Ah, I
want to thank you falettinme be mice elf again . . .
thank you falettinme be mice elf again . . .

Sly and the Family Stone blasting, followed by Nina Simone screaming "Sinner Man" and Al Green wanting to stay together. It was my kind of party. My employer, Corey, the photographer, had invited me to one of his parties. It was at his railroad loft on Twenty-sixth Street across from a parking garage and sandwiched between a Korean grocer and a wholesale fabric trim place. I spent a good deal of my work life in this studio, with its grungy kitchen, a tiny bathroom and a large living space where a red velvet couch and gold gilt headboard anchored the room. A Jackson Pollock dominated the main wall; photographs covered the rest of the walls. Being in this apartment felt like seeing a home I'd have one day, with its mismatched colors and crazy green walls. It was all so creative, so out there, so me.

I had run into Jay on Eighth Street in the Village and invited him. He was in grad school at NYU at the time, I was dealing with my mother's undiagnosed dementia and Zackie, who had reappeared, was plagued with various infections. I was feeling happy about work, but rootless in my personal life. The party was full of photographers, other assistants, booking agents and a general assortment of bourgeois bohemians like me. I danced till my clothes—cotton shirt and a very mini-skirt—were wet. At one point I looked over at Jay wedged between a woman with cobalt blue-and-black streaked hair talking with a photographer who'd done a celebrated exhibit on road kill. Jay looked like he belonged anyplace else, but he was engaging these two in what seemed to be a lively conversation. I had one of those feelings then, the kind that shoots through you, starting in your stomach and moves up to your head. In my mind, I see my parents in front of the sign that marked the entrance to their small southern college. They met in the late fifties, got married in '62; my dad, Lenny West (no one called him Leonard), had on a straw pork pie hat, Ray-Ban sunglasses and a toothpick dangling from between his lips. Mom, with a head full of that Eleazer hair, looks forlorn. She's smiling, but her eyes say something else—ensnared resignation. You can almost smell the hint of tobacco in the air along with manure and honeysuckle. It's early spring, but the weather is already warm, probably in the eighties. She's wearing a diaphanous blouse that looks white in the black-

and-white photograph, and checked clam diggers, the pants they now call capris. She's leaning into my dad, her hip bumping him away like some kind of cartoon character. His face is open; his grin is wide and pure. His arm is around her shoulder. He loves her, called her his filly. I never understood why when I was little. I do now. That filly is inside all Eleazer women.

My mother is pleading with me. "Don't be afraid, just be *you*. Everything will work out."

When I wasn't with my boss and his crowd, I hung out with Jay. He was living in NYU campus housing. When I was with him we had a pleasant, calm time. We did simple things, movies, low-key restaurants. He was wanting serious, I was testing, but leaning away from him, feeling sure I needed to figure out me first but also needing someone stable because of all that was happening with my mother and Zackie.

My boss had a show at a gallery in Alphabet City. I was serving wine on a tray, eavesdropping on comments from the very hippest photo people in the city. Jay had come with a friend from school, so I didn't feel like I had to entertain him. He seemed to be enjoying the exhibit. In walked Zackie, looking great, with a short, very guylike haircut, a sweater and jeans. He'd recently been released from the hospital. We hugged for a long time and found a corner where we could talk and he told me that he was very sick, some kind of cancer, and he didn't know how much longer he'd be well enough to walk around on his own. I felt myself stifling tears; actually thinking if I didn't cry then what he said wasn't true. I drank a cup of white

wine from the tray that now sat in my lap. If I didn't acknowledge it, it wasn't so. I put my hand on his and
promised to help him through whatever it was.

"You can't be sick. You're too young and too fabulous."
I was trying to be him, let him see himself in me and snap
out of it.

"You're my favorite," he said wearily.

Almost a year to the day after that show in Alphabet
City, I went to the hospital to see him. He was so thin that
his head looked enormous and his skin was pulled across
his face so tight you could see the bumps in his bones. He
smiled when I walked in with a pot of mums—an inside
family joke that the Eleazer sisters could only have flowers, like mums, that were as tough as they were.

He patted the part of bed next to him, as if to say, *sit
down, sit down.*

I put the flowers on the nightstand and sat. The nurses
had me put a mask over my face, gloves on my hands and
wear a gown.

"I'm so glad to see you," he said, his breathing rattled.

I'd had so many questions, things to say before getting
there.

Now seeing him, seeing just how bad it was, I sat mute.

"They say its pneumonia. Young people don't die of
pneumonia," he said.

"Of course, you'll get better," I said.

"I could, only to get sick again. But I'll take it. How're
you doing?"

"I'm fine, I love my job and living in the city and . . ."

"What's up with that Jay?"

"I know. He's kinda corny, huh?"

"Yes, but that's not what I was going to say. He's an ambitious one."

"You talked to him?"

"Quite a bit, at the opening."

"Well?"

"Ina Paris, that boy gonna be somebody, I just don't know whether he's the somebody for you."

Anyone who ever came into contact with Jay understood fairly soon that he was on fire.

"He adores you."

"I know," I said with a frown.

"Darling, that's never anything to be sad about."

"I know, but he's a little like Dad."

"Ain't nothin' wrong with Uncle Lenny, beats crazy-ass Ben hands down."

Daddy would love Jay. He'd approved of him completely, respected a young black man like him, a man who "goes for the brass ring, sugar." My dad remained in good physical and mental shape by running every day, eating oatmeal and not letting anything bother him. He'd wanted a gaggle of kids; something my mother had no interest in. He loved her and didn't seem bothered by the idea that he didn't understand her, he liked that she was her own person, even when she acted out he still liked her, liked her fire.

"Yeah, but I don't want that now," I said.

"You don't know what you want, Ina Paris," Zackie said, before dozing off for a nap.

*　　*　　*

So much of life is about letting go of illusions. I'd let go of mine after a night out with my boss. We're at a bar, some cruddy place that has rapidly vanished from Chelsea as it became chic. He used to like to go and drink Rolling Rocks and talk about art and commerce and photography. I liked being with him because I felt cool and so outside the box. I was playing pool with some guys I didn't know. We were all drinking and having fun. One of them and I discovered we lived near each other and decided to share a cab uptown. When we got to my place he told me he didn't have his key and didn't want to wake up his roommate, so could he just sack out on my couch? I had a studio with a sofa bed and a futon so I said sure, no problem. Even though I didn't know him, Corey, my boss, knew him, so I figured I was safe. I made up the sofa bed for him, went into my bathroom and put on flannels, socks and a bathrobe. Came out, said good night, crawled onto my futon. He gets up and comes over to me and starts kissing me. I tell him while I think he's nice, I'm seeing someone and don't want to do anything. He persists, pushing his face on mine and kissing me in the mouth even as I try to move my head away from his. The force of this sends my inner alarm that he's going to try to take what he wants. He's on top of me and pressing all his weight on me, I punch at his bulbous upper arms and try to wiggle from underneath his tremendous weight so I can knee him in the nuts. I can't move him. He presses, pulling down my pajama pants as I bite his shoulder and dig my nails into his arms. I feel like a child, like Tweetie Bird trying to fight Paul Bunyan, but I don't give up trying to fight. I pinch and squirm and bite and scratch until he stops bucking. We both lay there exhausted for different reasons. A tear rolls out of my eye into my ear. Hate mixed with shame fills my mouth. He gets up, buckles the belt of his black jeans and leaves.

I lay there, thinking what I should do, whom I can call. I want to call Zackie but it hurts to move and what could he do from a hospital bed? The insides of my forearms are sore and streaked red, my insides are sticky and hurt. I want to wash myself but I can't move. I stay there, my pajama pants still wrapped around my knees, my bathrobe opened and pushed under my arms, my socks off from trying to use my feet for leverage, to push him off. I stay there until the next day turns dark again. I don't answer the phone; I don't go to the bathroom. I do nothing. I do not move until Jay shows up at my apartment, worried because he couldn't get me on the phone and my boss said I didn't show up for work and hadn't called, which was not like me. By the time Jay came I'd pulled up my pajamas and told him that I was sick with a bad cold, just needed to stay in bed for a few days. He stayed with me, getting me food and studying at my tiny kitchen table. After that I was scared to be in my apartment alone, so I moved into Jay's, a hovel nicer than mine.

I quit my job, but not before using my medical coverage to see a doctor to make sure I wasn't pregnant or infected with anything transmittable. I didn't want to tell my boss what happened, didn't want to see him to be reminded of what had happened. I just told him that I needed to take care of family things, my mother and Zackie. I took temp jobs, working as a secretary at various faceless companies—wholesale women's clothing company, a glove manufacturer, a law office. A year later Jay graduated and got a job with a Manhattan real estate firm. I married him the day after he'd completed his six-month probationary stint at his firm, two months pregnant and petrified of who I was. We were twenty-six. We moved to the edge of Brooklyn Heights, had Malcolm, I became a stay-at-home mommy who breastfed till he was practically talking in sentences; made his food from organic ingredients; strained his juice; took long strolls to make sure he got enough vitamin D and fresh air; read for a half hour at night; enrolled in Baby and Me, then Toddler and Me and on and on. I was chic with my casual Gap/Banana Republic clothing. I joined a mothers' group with other stay-at-home mothers, all "used to bes," management consultants, architects, journalists, lawyers, book editors, all white women except Paula Sweet, who had invited me to join. I showed up, Malcolm on my hip, at Jackie's, a used-to-be banker. She lived on the parlor floor of a brownstone and had twin girls named Isabel and Madeline. When I walked in there were mothers and babies everywhere on the floor, each on their blanket or activity mat. Most of the babies were between five and nine months and Malcolm and I were desperate for social interaction. Paula got up from the floor with her baby boy Max and greeted me warmly.

"Oh, you came. Everyone," she said, clasping her hands, getting their attention.

"This is Ina and Malcolm. They're new to the Heights and Ina's a," she paused and looked at me, "photographer." I said used to be in my head but nothing out loud.

"And her husband Jay is doing real estate at Stevens and Chang," she nodded her chin in one downward motion as if to say, *you all know the firm.* "Okay, that's it. Oh, and Malcolm is seven months."

Paula turned to me.

"Get something to eat. Jackie's a fabulous cook. Try the ratatouille. I can hold Malcolm or you can just put him down, her space is totally baby-proofed."

I was hungry all the time. It was amazing how much energy nursing took. I carried Malcolm over to the dining room table where everything was casually laid out—bagels, breads sliced, tomatoes, capers, tuna and chicken salad and the ratatouille in a Crock-Pot. I fixed myself a bowl and grabbed a piece of garlic toast, my mouth thrilling to the anticipation, and then I realized I couldn't eat tomatoes, too acidic in the breast milk. I put it aside and quickly smeared chicken salad on a bagel, practically inhaling it. I looked into the living room and it looked like a map with each baby and mom on a separate island. The mothers of older babies were better dressed, hair combed with even a little makeup. All were intently interacting with their babies and chatting with each other. I saw Jackie and decided she was a good place to start. She was small with dark straight hair and dark rectangular glasses.

"He's adorable," she said, as I sat down next to her.

"Thanks."

"He sleeping?"

Meaning, is he sleeping through the night yet?

"Not great. How about yours?"

"You know twins are a lot, but in some ways they're easier."

"You're kidding."

"Well, identical ones, anyway, are so tuned into each other, they seem to need me less."

I looked at them sitting, facing each other, touching one another's face.

"You gonna have more?" she asked.

"I don't know. We're just getting used to this one."

"Ah yes, the first one knocks the hell out of you. They say the second one's easier. So how do you know Paula?"

"From my book club."

"Do your husbands know each other?"

"No. Why?"

"No, I just, um, it's just everybody here pretty much knows each other through the husbands, you know, since none of us work anymore . . ."

The women were friendly enough. I learned the topics stayed pretty much on the babies' milestones, whose pediatrician was understanding, foods to try, what's gassy, complaints about what the husbands didn't understand and what they didn't do when Mom finally got a break on a weekend afternoon—forgot to feed the baby, change him, walk her. The mommy group was like being part of a remote village—those afternoons we'd spend nursing our babies without covering ourselves, sitting around on pillows on the floor, eating, talking, knowing that we all knew exactly how tired tired was. Jay was building his career and getting bigger and bigger every year, he worked constantly. He was out the door as Malcolm and I awoke and came home after we were both long asleep. The mommy group had become our salvation. When Malcolm was three and a half, I got pregnant again and Jay decided we needed to live around more black people and that Malcolm and soon-to-be Marcus should live in a house with a backyard, so we moved to Pomona.

We found our perfect house, in the fancy part of Pomona, where Jay always wanted to live. He believed it was as good a small city as any. He grew up yearning for a life on the hill, to walk to the pretentiously unpretentious shops and be greeted by name. He liked having an account at the wine shop, where the owner would send over a case of a vintage he thought Jay might like. He liked living in a place where he'd been an Eagle Scout, a lettered baseball player. Jay's younger brother was a fireman in Pomona but lived far enough away, in Pennsylvania; steering clear of their father. Jay was determined to live his illusion. And no one talked about Jay's dad—who folks in the Hollow knew hung out on Mission Street, clutching a bottle in a paper bag, the thing that had cost him his family and his job at sanitation. It was the one thing about Jay that I didn't understand. I'd think he would want to be as far from Pomona and his dad as possible and whenever I tried to get him to talk about it, he would just say it wasn't an issue for him.

My attempts at an unconventional life had hurt me and scared me and while I knew Jay's route of club women teas, *House Beautiful* homes, shopping as an Olympic sport and social busyness were all distractions to keep the ennui at bay, to keep conversations with that real self away, the one who you were before you got hurt, lost first prize, discovered you didn't have the energy to fight for who you really wanted to become, I'd accepted it all. And for thirteen years the little murky world visible only to the people who are part of it was enough. And it still was enough for many of the people I knew. At my book club, there was always just one complaint; husbands worked too many long hours and when they weren't working played too much golf. I told myself that his golf was like my mommy's group had been for me. A refuge. Plus if Jay hadn't taken up golf, I'm sure I would've left him. Having him around was much worse than not because he was constant motion, talking, needing. I liked the peace, before we had Ivy and when the boys were occupied and I could read or take a walk or on some really good days take my camera out and shoot a roll of just squirrels or leaves or grass. Once, after we'd had the basement refinished and Jay insisted on putting in a dark room for me, I did a series of self-portraits with my hair in different incarnations: picked out in a huge Afro, cornrows, blown straight. Mom thought they were great and commented, probably for the first time, certainly the first time that I remembered, that I really did have *something*. Jay asked me what the point was. When I didn't answer him, he said, "I guess I just don't get it, as usual."

I didn't use the dark room again.

Jay wanted me to show my work, develop as a photographer and contact my old boss, and I realized later that I resented him for it. How come he didn't just intuit that something horrible had happened? I was doing all that taking care of things, all that I never got from my mother, overdoing—I now admit—and I didn't have any energy left over for taking pictures or getting better. I was busy trying to kill the illusion.

avid and I had had a crucial thing in common: We'd both been raised by mothers who were ghosts. His mother a big-time lawyer turned child advocate; mine an art teacher and a frustrated painter. My mother's job at the school, her long drives to clear her head, her friends, her sisters all seemed to come before me. She made the time for them, not for me. While she was dutiful with the public things—made cookies for the bake sales at school, showed up for parent-teacher conferences, she'd never just flop down and play Barbie or color or play jacks or just hold me in her lap to read a book together. Never. After a while I stopped asking her to. I just did my own thing, in my head. I know now that I was wiring my own mother tack to be different, more involved, more hands-on, just more. Now I've done that with mine, I've literally given them my life and I can no longer breathe because I'm dying. Maybe this drowning is the very thing that my own mother was so afraid of.

David's mother was busy, very busy with her career. It was more than a career. Her children's aide society was a mission. I remember meeting her for the first time like it happened today. *All children are my children. We can't leave one by the wayside. Our success is the success of our children.* These things just rolled out of her mouth, as if she were always giving a speech. Her tall and elegant body, patchouli-scented, was always wrapped in some flowing luxurious fabrics, like silk and velvet. I thought of her as a queen.

David and I had been dating a few months when he had invited me home one Sunday for their ritual Sunday brunch. We drove up from Howard through Rock Creek Park into the hills of what the locals call the Platinum Coast. Their house, elegantly reserved, sat slightly back on a hill. Volvos and Saabs, early models, lined the driveway. Her jewelry, of which she wore a lot, all had a story. Lots of gold, given to her by various African women elders, an ivory bracelet from an early trip to Mozambique, a ruby-encrusted choker from members of the Congressional Black Caucus for her work in establishing national full-day preschool.

David's presence at brunch was required, as was his father's. Other guests from the embassies or universities or government, the arts, were like a rotating assortment on a lazy Susan. The variety pleased David's mother. She loathed boredom.

"So Ina, are you enjoying D.C.?" she asked me as we sat with plates on our laps on a settee in the dining room.

"Um, yeah, it's such a pretty city, although I don't get off campus very much."

"You like Howard?"

"I do."

"I did, too. What're you majoring in?"

I wanted to say "David," but he saved me from myself by interrupting.

"Ma-ah, that's enough," David said, fixing his plate at the breakfront.

"Oh darling, I'm just getting to know Ina. Do you feel like I'm prying, sweetheart? Tell the truth."

I felt heat coming from her, like rays off a star. I loved the attention, being this close to her where I could smell her fragrant skin. I looked at her long face, brilliant cinnamon-colored skin, and sparkling eyes and thought, She can ask me anything. I was totally smitten by her.

"No, not at all," I said.

David's father, a hefty, distinguished-looking man with a bald head with salt-and-pepper sides, sat at the head of the table, drinking coffee and chuckling.

"Perhaps next time you come, Ina, you'll remember to just bring your curriculum vitae," he said, sounding like a professor played by Roscoe Lee Browne.

"Oh Milford, stop it," David's mother said, laughing, too.

She took a few breaths and continued her questioning. I wondered how much David had told her about me, if he'd told her anything at all.

"So what are you majoring in?"

"Right now theater arts but I'm thinking about changing."

"To?"

"Um, something else in fine arts, maybe photography. I'm not sure."

"Well, what do you enjoy? You should major in whatever you're passionate about."

"Tell that to my mother," I mumbled but she heard me and agreed.

"Ah yes, she wants something practical for you?"

"Basically. I think she's just scared."

"Of course. It goes with the territory, I'm afraid."

I had a pleasant time, stuffing myself and sipping champagne.

When we left I was happy and tipsy. David was quiet and seemed annoyed.

"I liked your parents," I said after riding in silence for a few minutes.

"Yeah, they're just swell."

I was surprised that he seemed so irritable. I mentally went through the afternoon, trying to figure out what had bothered him.

"Are you upset?"

I felt panic in my insides. We'd been dating for two semesters and had declared ourselves in love. This was the first bump we'd hit.

"Um, yes, Ina. I'm upset."

The alarm intensified as it would for a nineteen-year-old girl who's getting her affirmation from a twenty-three-year-old guy.

We got to my dorm and he pulled into the circular driveway, failing to turn off the car or even take his foot off the clutch.

"You're not coming up?"

He sighed and said he had too many papers to grade.

"I'll talk to you tomorrow."

No, David, you'll talk to me now, I wanted to demand. Instead I just grabbed my denim bag off the floor and got out.

In the elevator to my floor, crowded with kids coming in from Georgetown, the library, evening chapel, I crossed my arms around myself, holding myself so I would hold back my tears. I quickly walked to my room and unlocked my door. I threw my bag and myself onto my batik-covered twin bed and cried into my pillow. After a few minutes I fell into a subterranean alcohol-induced sleep.

I overslept the next day and had to skip a shower in order to make it to my nine o'clock anthropology class. I opened my door, tripping over a plant and a note from David: *It's not you. It's them. I'm sorry.*

Fifteen years later David was sitting on the couch listening to music with headphones on, conducting with a pencil. I stood in front of him to get his attention, having made the calls to check on my children. He removed the headset and patted the sofa. I sat down next to him. It was the closest I'd been to him since seeing him. The heat was still there and it felt delicious and uncomfortable. He put his arm around me and touched my chin with his finger.

"You look fantastic, like a woman now."

I can't.

He removed his arm and held them up as if to surrender.

"Cool."

*   *   *

I had become one of those people who finish Christmas shopping before Thanksgiving. But this year, I hadn't bought one gift. Hadn't processed how I'd do everything without Jay: get the lights on the house, put the sleigh on the lawn, get the tree. I hadn't even figured out how we'd get through the day without Jay and what I would tell the kids about that. I was finally going to have to tell them the truth. I'm sure Malcolm knew the truth anyway. He was always like that, like he could smell what I was thinking.

I got myself dressed and went downstairs to David's kitchen. I'd been away from home for almost a week and was feeling rejuvenated and anxious, guilty and lonely. I missed my kids but wasn't in the mood to dive right back into that pool of sadness, deceptions and just feeling bad about myself, comparing myself to the fabulous phantom Julie Jarvis. I bet she had a flat stomach, too. But I couldn't stand the thought of inflicting permanent damage on my children with my sudden disappearance.

David had left for work and the house was blissfully silent. I straightened up a little—out of habit more than anything, washed up the breakfast dishes and coffee mugs, swept the floor, put the trash out. Sweeping is right up there with meditation for getting to the root of things. While I'd been a dutiful wife, I hadn't been a very passionate one and I don't mean in bed, I mean giving a shit about Jay's daily life. I made sure his creature comfort was just right, but sort of neglected what was really going on with him. The same way I'd neglected my own inner life. I guess that's why people leave marriages, have affairs—they meet somebody else who fills in where the spouse used to be before he or she got so preoccupied with running all the stuff they thought they were building for each other—the career, house, the kids, getting the dog to the vet. I had to just sit down.

Jay and I had a four-gift maximum for each child, which I adhered to and he never did. They had so much stuff already but he couldn't keep himself from buying more. "Hell, Ina, we can afford it." I made them pack up the stuff they no longer played with and took it to a homeless shelter. I couldn't even remember what the boys had wanted or what Ivy liked. These were things Jay did. He knew what they liked, remembered the toys they talked about back in the summer months. I put my elbows on the pine table and my face into my hands and just sobbed. David's phone rang once, stopped and rang again. Our code.

"What's up?"

I didn't respond.

"You alright?"

"Yeah, yeah. I'm okay. I'm going to have to go home."

"Today?" he said, sounding alarmed.

"Uh, yeah. I gotta get back to my kids."

Silence.

"Oh yeah. Of course."

"Christmas is coming and I haven't even shopped yet and I gotta figure out what to tell them . . ."

"Okay, well . . ."

I could tell David was becoming bored with the details

of my life; buying toys for three kids was something that couldn't possibly interest him and he didn't want to deal with the Jay stuff at all.

"You think you could wait till I get home?"

This surprised me.

"Um, yeah, yeah, I can leave after you get home, another few hours won't make much difference."

"Good. I'll see you around seven."

I hung up the phone and was almost immediately sorry that I'd made him that promise. I wouldn't get home until after midnight. The last thing I wanted was time on my hands to think about what was awaiting me. I could start my shopping down here, I suppose. That would surely kill a couple hours and I could call Leelah, maybe she could meet for lunch or something.

It felt weird being back in D.C. like this, driving around, doing errands. In some ways it felt as if I'd never left. The way people spoke—the regular folk—saying double *rr*s in a way that continued to crack me up: married was *marred*; terrible was *terrbul*; Maryland was *Merrlyn*. It was a place unto itself, all those black folks. I'd forgotten how strange that was at first and how I had come to love it. It was like being in another country, just seeing black people everywhere.

After I'd bought each child two presents I was worn out and hungry and thought I'd take a chance on catching Leelah for lunch. She was in her office eating already but had a few hours free before her next class, so I went to campus to meet her.

"There's a Starbucks right down the street," she said as we crossed the campus.

"There's so much new stuff here now, all of Georgia Avenue, it looks like . . ." I said.

"Welcome to the new Howard, honey."

We laughed as we walked arm-in-arm to Georgia Avenue, seeing young, gorgeous kids with dreadlocks and perms and funky clothes and straight ones brought my memories of college back for me. A few of them nodded, acknowledging Professor Vance or just to the two "older" yet still attractive women. Was I actually old enough to be considered "older"? My hair was in a recent style, teeth not too yellow? I hadn't actually noticed myself aging. I was just living, but now seeing these coeds and their low-slung jeans, tight waistlines, high behinds I realized I'd become middle-aged, half my life already lived.

"Where does the damn time go?" I said out loud, but really talking to myself.

"*Humph.* I know. Amazing, isn't it. We were just there. Everything seemed so important then, remember? Whom you were going out with, acing the final, dealing with your roommate . . ."

"We must have had the two worst roommates on campus!"

We laughed the kind of familiar laugh one has with old friends. Being with Leelah was as warm and sweet as sipping hot chocolate on a cold February day wrapped in a chenille throw.

"So what's going on?" Leelah started after we sat down with our Venti lattes.

"I'm going home today . . . I've gotta get back and take care of my kids."

"Of course. Who have they been with?"

"My folks and my neighbor. My neighbor has a lotta help. She saves my life."

"So you don't have a nanny or a housekeeper?"

"Nope. I did for a while, when I was working, but you talk about drama, there's always something with these nannies and after four or five, I just figured I'd do it all myself. Then it became this badge I wore in my town where people have people to do everything for them. It's just become who I am . . ."

"Sweetie, you still need to take some time to take care of you. Anybody can run a vacuum and cook."

I knew it was the truth, but I'd just been on autopilot for so long, I didn't know what anything else looked like.

I was just determined to be everything for my kids, including cooking and cleaning for them. I looked at her and felt pissed at her but didn't want to deal with those feelings, didn't want to have them.

"Oh, I do things. I have my book club, I . . ."

"Uh-huh, but what about your photography, your art? The stuff that gives your soul some meaning."

I looked into the dwindling foam and felt my nose begin to burn.

Leelah rubbed the top of my hand. She knew. She always knew.

"I ask myself that a hundred times a day. How did I get here? What happened to the person I used to be? And how do I get her back?"

"I don't know if you want the old person back, at least not all of her, but there has to be some way to incorporate the old her and the new. I mean, I understand you have responsibilities now. I also know that this motherhood thing is huge, so much bigger than anybody ever tells you and if they do, you can't know till you're in it."

"Tell me about how you got Luka."

"He's Cindy's baby. You remember my sister Cindy?"

I nodded.

"Seems she couldn't handle the mother-wife thing and just packed up one day, left her husband a note and was outta there."

"Wow. She just left?"

"Yep, I know it's hard to imagine, but she did."

It wasn't that hard. I could certainly understand feeling overwhelmed.

"How'd she go about it? I mean . . ."

"She packed up Luka, he was six months and brought him to my parents' house and said Larry, her husband, would be picking him up. Of course, Larry didn't know anything about this. He was at work and when he got home he found a note from her saying she was moving to L.A. to realize her potential."

"Well, how'd you end up with the baby?"

"Larry's a nice guy, but he couldn't handle a baby and my parents are too old. He just wasn't the type to take it on. He was very straightforward about it. He sends checks every month, but he's never been comfortable with the parental thing. I think he loved Cindy and just wanted to give her what she said she wanted . . ."

I sat sipping my latte as Leelah talked and thought about my own marriage and kids. I'd fantasized more than once about leaving Jay with the kids. When we were at a point where everything he did annoyed the hell out of me, whether it was eating potato salad with his mouth opened or trying to kiss me good night with bad breath or just his jocund presence, all of it just began to make me feel like running, running out of there, but I never would've. I wouldn't have been able to leave my kids.

"Does anybody hear from her?"

Leelah took a sip and then another.

"*Mmm*, this is good . . . um, sure. She calls, I guess once a month. We send her pictures. She wants to know how he is, but she also wants to be free. She works out, Rollerblades around Santa Monica, goes on auditions and works as a waitress."

"You think she's happy?"

Leelah looked at me and pulled her tortoiseshell glasses down her nose.

"I think she's satisfied. What the hell is happy? Who's happy? And what does that have to do with anything?"

"Oh, stop being a philosopher for five minutes, please. You know what the hell I mean."

She pushed her glasses back up and then took them off. Without makeup and a blazer she looked seventeen.

"I know what you mean, but really I think as we get older happy is just not a construct we need to be chasing. The more substantial thing is what we generate and that's more a feeling of contentment, feeling fulfilled."

"I know, I know . . ."

"Do you? Really?"

"Why do I feel like you're getting at something? I'm not

in your class. You don't have to show off for me. I'm sure you're very good at what you do."

It came out more hostile than I intended. I didn't realize that I was envious of how she had it all together—a career, a baby, a lover, herself and I couldn't seem to put on pantyhose and tie my shoes properly.

We sat in silence for a while.

"So do you wanna talk about what's really going on?"

I was tired and I gave her a look that let her know that.

"What do you want me to say? That I'm sitting here hating you because you've pulled off something I can't."

"Ina, that's not true."

"Well, it certainly looks that way."

"Nobody's life is perfect."

"I have to get back and pack."

"Ina, don't leave like this."

She looked at me and I looked away.

"I'll be in touch."

I got back to David's just as it was becoming dark, still several hours before he was due to be home. I climbed the creaking stairway and began to pack my things. Coming here, trying to reclaim something, was probably a bad idea. It had just made me feel worse, especially seeing what successes David and Leelah had become. It highlighted my feelings of being a failure. Who needed it? What was wrong with me? It was like I was in some kind of a coma, numbingly going along with what I thought Jay wanted, which was a woman who looked like me, but had no inner life. A woman who just wanted a man to go out and make a thick check and buy jewelry and take nice vacations and throw big parties for all the people we knew to come and be impressed by the big house and beautiful furnishings. Get your hair done and edit the interesting person out of yourself. The thing is, I did it willingly; I became that girl that he never asked for.

Just as I began wrapping my toothbrush in a plastic bag I heard David's door slam.

He called my name from downstairs, again, like we were an old married couple. Suddenly I imagined what it would've been like to have married David, precious David. Why hadn't I just stayed with him, tried to work things out if what I told myself was true? If he had been my love, the big love of my life. And why hadn't he tried to find me in all those years? The stairs squeaked at each pounding footstep.

"You're early," I said.

"Yeah. I didn't want you to sneak out without saying good-bye," he said, entering the guest room.

He'd read my mind.

David walked toward me looking like a warm piece of pecan pie with whipped cream. His caramel cheeks were a little blushed from the freezing December day, his pumpkin-colored scarf blending nicely with his camel overcoat.

"I'm glad you came to see me."

"Are you? I'm not so sure it was such a good idea," I said, zipping up my bag.

I could feel his breath on my face.

"I gotta . . ."

He put his hands on my face and pulled me toward him.

He brushed his lips across my face before stopping at my
mouth, open and hungry for him.

We kissed each other hard and long, fingers through
hair, ears, cheeks, necks. I could feel his body pressing
mine. The bed right there at our side, but I resisted. I
knew if I let myself fall, I might not get up again. I wasn't
prepared for what might happen, what could.

"David, David," I said, trying to awaken him from his
passionate daze.

He slowly stopped kissing me, but held my face gently
in his palms.

"Why didn't you ever come after me? All that time . . ."

He took his hands away from my face and took my
hands in his.

"I honestly don't know. I could tell you all the things I
was doing to fill up my days, my time. My career. I had
other women, you know that, but I never wanted to make a
real commitment to any of them and most of them were
just great. It was me. Being contrary doesn't make it easy
to find a mate. I don't know, most of the time I don't think I
really wanted one. But you . . ."

"But me what? If I had hung on I would've been another
one who was just great but. I would've been hanging on,
waiting for you to commit. You know that as well as I do."

"Ina, you know what we had. You were the only one."

"But I'm married now. I have three children. I come
with a lot of extras now."

"I'd take it all. We could have another one, together."

I took a breath for what felt like the first time since he'd
kissed me.

"David, I have to go home."

"I know, I know. You go home. Think about what I said. Take care of what you have to. I'm not going anywhere."

He looked at me deeply, his eyes saying, *I'm for real.* Mine saying, *I doubt you and I don't have time to deal with this now.*

I picked up my bag.

"Thanks for being here."

He kissed me on my cheek.

He walked me to my SUV, put my bag in the back. I got in the driver's seat, handed him his key, checked the CDs in the player, getting my driving music ready: Patti La-Belle, Guy, Howard Hewitt and always Chaka.

"I will love anyway, even if you cannot stay . . ."

For me it's Chaka. I loved her in college for her irreverence and still do, for her strength and resilience and for all the seeming contradictory things she is—an R&B princess with all the stuff that went with that kind of life, especially in the seventies. . . . the hair, the lips, the fur jeans. She would scream the beat if she felt like it, just doing her own thing and not giving a shit whether you liked it or got it.

I took off heading north to face the pain, Chaka egging me on.

CHAPTER TWELVE

L ast year Jay and I had made this drive, coming back from Howard's homecoming weekend. Just last year we were gathered at the annual alumni reunion for the spectacle football game, parties and catching up. A lot of marriages were made at Howard. Classic stories: fell in love sophomore year, broke up junior year, got back together second semester, senior year, married after grad school; had the first baby second year of marriage. Those folks, like us, came back to homecoming with children and nannies in tow, wanting their heirs to develop a taste for life at the "Mecca." Even those who married other graduates of elite black colleges did the same thing, these schools were an extension of one another for the pageantry was similar—the Greek Step Show; the generations of Howard grads hobbling across campus, looking for their banner class of 1935, '45, '55; the Best of

Friends, the reunion party for mostly latter-day baby boomers, fabulous-looking black people gathered from everywhere from Sausalito to Sarasota in one place, squealing at the sight of each other. It was a network at which AT&T would marvel. At any place in the U.S. or abroad you could reach out and connect with another Howard grad. Even when you didn't like somebody, there was a level of familial pride in an alum's accomplishments. It was like another universe, with a unique language, uniforms and customs; you'd chosen and come through a place most of the population either doesn't know exists or discounts because they don't get it. Some white people wonder why one would want to go to school with all blacks—didn't y'all fight for the right to go to school with us; some black folks feel like black colleges are either inferior or "unrealistic because you don't learn how to deal with white folks." The reality is *au contraire*. It's probably the first, and maybe the only time, you get to forget about race. When you all look alike, you can move on to other things—character becomes the only important thing. If you like someone or don't it's because of who they are, not the preconceptions of who they are based on race. Prof gives you a bad grade, you don't have to even go to a place of *did I get this because I'm black?*

Jay, like everybody else, liked to go back to get reaffirmed. He got his dose from his frats who seemed to spend all their time together assuring one another that "you the man, no, *you* the man." I was glad to be there with Jay, having thought I'd put David into a steamer trunk with the rest of my past, somewhere in the attic out of sight. And I knew he'd *never* come to a homecoming. It had been more than a few years since I'd gone. Jay usually went without me to relive his time with his frat brothers, show off, without the wife nagging him about drinking too much or talking too loud or spending too much money. But this year I decided to go and look for Leelah, who I'd lost touch with.

I mingled through the entire ballroom, *How can that be, where'd the time go. You still look great, you haven't changed; I put on a little weight, hell, who hasn't? But considering everything, you look great. How's it going? How's your life?* Everyone came back for the Best of Friends party, where there would be enough late-seventies early-eighties music to soak everyone's designer outfits. We could go back for a night to when we were beautiful and oh-so-sure of our stellar futures. When we knew our accomplishments would be chronicled in *Black Enterprise, The New York Times* and the *Smithsonian.* We'd conquer disease, write hit plays and argue before the Supreme Court. We'd show at MoMA, dance on Broadway, run companies. This is what was expected, not the exception for a true Howardite. We were the ones to take it to the next level . . . "Ain't No Stoppin Us Now," was our theme song. Success was as expected, as was hearing "One Nation Under a Groove" and the crowd going wild on the ballroom floor of the Washington Hilton. Many of us were still beautiful or at least we were that night. Outfits were expensive and well thought out. Husbands hassled their wives to look their best, knowing that impressing that old girlfriend who got away was crucial.

There was one in particular I noticed. The philosophy major—Leelah—had broken his heart on the quad, left him in little pieces for his Nupes to put back together. But he was big-time on Wall Street now, stories regularly written about him appeared in *Fortune* and the *Wall Street Journal* and the *New York Times* business section. He'd made so much money it wasn't even discussed anymore, had been making it for the last fifteen. He was *the man* and a big contributor to Howard, his Ivy League business school, his fraternity and his child's Manhattan day school and still appeared to be just a nice boy from Ohio, even though he was already in possession of a new trophy wife. His first, a Miss Dorm 1979, had been tossed on the heap of first wives after it was clear sailing into enough millions where even dividing wouldn't hurt too much. She'd been the rebounder anyway, when Leelah told him no thanks to his proposal on graduation eve. While Leelah, the philosophy major who was now a philosophy professor, was still beautiful even undone, was at the party with her girlfriend and child, blissfully ignorant of all this as she didn't even read the financial news. She saw him and wife number two, a tiny ball of anxious energy who looked and acted like a black Parker Posey. He walked over to Leelah and I watched the whole thing from across the lobby. Saw her come in dressed, as usual, against the grain. It was a black-tie event and Leelah was in loose beige jersey pants and a fitted khaki green quilted vest. Her hair, which was always searching for a style, was simply pulled up in a loose topknot, with strands casually flying free on her neck and temples. She looked beautiful.

"Hey Ed," she said, loudly as she hugged him tight, "How you doin'?" He hugged her back, awkwardly, as the wife stood impatiently nearby his six-foot, five-inch frame.

"How you been, Leelah?" he asked, moving back from her, taking the wife by the elbow.

"Great, great. Is this your wife?"

"Yes, this is . . ."

"Sheila. I'm Sheila Marshall," she stuck out her tiny hand, the big Lucinda diamond screaming.

"Oh Sheila, it's so nice to meet you."

They stood there in painful small talk for a few seconds before I came up, deciding Leelah needed to be rescued.

I had noticed the preppy woman standing next to her with a baby on her back. The woman, who looked like a smaller version of Leelah, turned and bent down so she could take the baby out of the pack. I made my way over and stood at the foot of the stairs and said her name.

"Ina. Ina West Robinson, is that you?" she said as she gave the baby back to the woman and made her way to me and I to her. We embraced for what had to be five minutes. We hugged and swayed and kissed each other's checks and wiped away tears.

"Oh, stop it now, don't do that," Leelah said to me, as she did the same thing.

"I've missed you so, more than I knew," I said.

We hugged some more until our bodies were warm from embracing so hard and long.

"And you have a baby?"

"Come meet them," she said, holding my hand, leading me over to the woman and baby who'd come into the hotel lobby with her.

"Ina, this is my partner, Serena. And this is Luka."

I extended my hand and smiled at Serena.

"It's nice to meet you."

"Oh, and Ed, Sheila, meet Serena."

They looked like they were in the middle of a third world coup and mumbled something about having to go. Leelah and Serena smiled graciously at them and said good-bye.

Serena turned to Leelah and they smiled a knowing one at each other.

"My goodness, look at this gorgeous child and look at these cheeks," I said.

Serena moved closer to me so I could get a better look, beneath his hat.

"I know, he eats nonstop, we figure he'll try out for the Redskins in a few more months," Serena said.

I turned my attention back to Leelah.

"So when did all this happen?"

She knew that I meant more than the baby.

"We have so much catching up to do. I've missed you, too, so much. I'd think about you, pick up the phone or write a letter and then just drop it," she said.

"Where are you living now?"

"I'm here, right in Adams Morgan. I left California after I finished my postdoc at Berkeley. I'm teaching at Howard."

"No fucking way. You? Miss I'll-never-step-foot-in-this-oppressive-ass-place-again-as-long-as-I-live . . . ?"

We laughed the familiar gut-level laugh. The one we'd shared so many times. We'd had our own thing since freshman orientation week. We were both in the quad with roommates who brought so much shit that it took up our space, too. We were both minimalists who'd been sent to Howard to "get our black on," from parents who felt strongly that one must first identify with one's tribe. We'd both had primarily private, white school experiences and weren't feeling negative about that but were ready for more flavor from our own. What we were bemused to find out was that there were many tribes at Howard, not just one. You had the Hinkty and the kinky and the revolutionary and the Buppie and the Greeks and the artists and the right-wingers and the five-percenters and the bohos from New York, who were different from the bohos from California, and of course you had your BAPs, men and women. Leelah and I felt strongly that we didn't fit into any mode. We were kind of boho, with a little bit of BAP and some wannabe intellectual/artist in there, too. We loved each other deeply.

"Listen we need to talk, but you know this isn't the place. Let's have brunch tomorrow, just us?"

"That'll be great," I said.

"How about Omega's? It's still there."

"Great. I need to go find Jay. I'll see you tomorrow."

I didn't sleep much that night. The conversation with Leelah just ran through my head—I played over and over what I wanted to say to her, what I wanted to tell her about how my life had been and how it was now. I didn't have a friend like her in my Pomona life. I had plenty of my children's friends' mothers who I was fond of or my PTA moms or even some others in the kids' social group, Ashley and Amir, but I didn't let any of those women really see me, all of me. I just felt so distanced from myself, perhaps because I had so many misplaced parts.

The next day Jay got up and out of the hotel to play ball with his frats. I took a long bath, grabbed a paper and got to the restaurant an hour early. I couldn't wait. I sipped a cup of Earl Grey tea while I waited.

Leelah came, also early, and we just smiled at each other. Catching up was going to take energy we both agreed, and preceded to order hearty breakfast food: grits, potatoes, biscuits, turkey sausage and cheese eggs.

"So I cannot believe you have a baby," I began.

"Why not? You have two . . ." she chuckled.

"Three, almost."

"You're pregnant?" Leelah practically screamed.

I looked around and I jokingly motioned to her to keep her voice down.

"How long? You're not showing . . ."

I pulled my top taunt across my belly.

"Almost six months and I *am* showing . . ."

"Oh yeah. That's great. Isn't motherhood just the best?"

"It is. It's a lot of work, but, yeah, it's wonderful."

"I can see how you just fall in love with these babies and you're just willing to do anything for them," Leelah said.

"Yes, my kids are my life."

Leelah shifted in her seat.

"What?"

"Nothing."

"Oh, say it, Leelah. We know each other too well . . ."

"Well, I just wasn't prepared to see you like this. I mean, you're so different."

"Like?"

"I don't know—you look different."

I was wearing my nice black pregnancy clothes, long-sleeved stretch cotton top and pull-on pants. My permed, bobbed hair was in a ponytail, which was totally different from my freer natural style.

"You just look so normal."

I put my fist to my chest to pretend to stab myself.

Something I used to run from.

Leelah looked at me, her deep-set eyes filled with compassion.

"I didn't mean to suggest . . . I've said too much."

"No, no, I want to hear it. I'm confused myself about what happened to me," I said.

"Well, what happened?"

"I don't know. I guess I just figured it was easier to cut out all those different parts."

"Just like that and become Martha," Leelah said and we both chuckled, although we knew this wasn't funny.

"Yeah, I just thought if I could organize my look and my home, make both beautiful and perfect enough that my life would be that way."

Leelah reached for my hand as sadness formed in her eyes.

"But you *were perfect*. All those straggly threads made you that way."

We spent the rest of the day together. Lingering in Omega's till they started putting chairs on the tables. We stumbled out of the cavelike café, shocked to find the sunshine dwindling. Walking around the formally funky Adams Morgan, ducking in and out of shops along Columbia Road. We just wanted to soak up the feelings of being together.

"So when did you come out?" I said, after giving up on coming up with something that was less of a cliché.

"I was wondering when we'd get to that . . ."

"You know it doesn't matter to me," I interrupted.

"Oh yeah, yeah. No—I know it's not an issue for you. I just know that you were surprised last night."

"Yeah, but last night I was distracted by Ed and his new, um, bride."

"Whoa . . . what was that about? Did you see him—all stiff, looking like the last tycoon. Eh, and that wife . . ."

"Well, you know he's like a billionaire?"

"No. I didn't and if that's what it looks like, let me stay broke. I took one look at the two of them and knew a second more in their presence was too much out of my life. What happened to sweet Ed Marshall?"

"He'd a turned out better if you hadn't rejected him."

We laughed so loud, a few people on the street looked toward us.

"Damn, that's my fault."

"So back to you . . ." I said.

"Oh yeah. Coming out. Let's see, I guess I came out in grad school."

"That long? Why didn't you tell me?"

"I don't know. It was weird. The first year or so, it was just hard to understand myself . . ."

"Did something happen?"

"You mean like a broken heart? A burning bush? No pun intended."

We laughed and she continued.

"You know, I'd had a few bad brothers—fine, brilliant, crazy, haven't we all— but I guess it occurred to me that every time I broke up with one of them, I never really felt bad. I didn't miss them cause they'd never really entered me."

"*Mmm*, entered, that's a good description," I said, and thought about Jay and David.

"That never happened and at that point, I'm like twenty-five, twenty-six and I'm starting to think maybe there's something up. I mean, I always knew I was different, but then, so are you, so are all the people I really like, so there was no need for me to think, different, gay."

"Yeah, that makes sense."

"Then I met somebody. A woman. Lauren."

"And it was love?"

"It was insanity, made me crazy. Thank God I met Serena, who is the essence of sanity and goodness, otherwise who knows what would've happened to me."

"What'd ya mean?"

"Oh girl. That's another long meal, for another day."

"Yeah, I need to get off my feet, get back to the hotel and pack up."

I hadn't noticed how long we'd been talking.

"When are you and Jay heading back?"

"Tonight. I have your number now."

"Yeah, we've found each other again. Let's hold on this time, okay?"

"I promise."

CHAPTER THIRTEEN

I got home around ten. The house shone like a beacon, the exterior spotlights had been turned on by a timer. I knew Ivy was asleep at Paige's and looking at her imposing white colonial with its striped awnings, I longed to see my baby's face. I'd have to wait till morning. I walked into my house, expecting to trip over the jumble of Nikes that were usually clustered around the door, but instead found a house that had been vacuumed and lemon-polished. The smell of Windex still hung in the air. Paige had sent in her forces.

I checked the stack of mail that had been neatly piled on the hall chest. I saw Ivy's walker tucked into a corner and ached to feel her pudgy cheek against mine, squeeze her little body while she put her chunky hands on my head, feeling the drool against my chin as she gave me a combination kiss-bite. I wanted to feel Marcus's wiry arms around my shoulders, his hugs less frequent, but no less intense; Malcolm, who is almost as tall as me and hugs me like a young man, but without reservation. They were my life and I'd needed time away from them.

After a reunion with my kids, where my boys greeted me coolly, I decided I needed some intelligence about Jay's girlfriend. He'd kept his word paying the bills and calling the boys daily, but he'd avoided talking to me. I made a lunch date with Kayreen Sparks, who had been our broker when we bought our house in Pomona and whom Jay hired when he opened his own office. She'd had to go to work after her basketball-playing husband dumped her for a Nets City dancer and she'd had to fight for child support. She was a southern belle who'd been sharpened by big-city life and having been the wife of a professional athlete. She became a gold producer and was still, deep under her Ungaro suits, a good southern girl. She had built a profitable real estate business, and bought part interest in our town paper. She knew everybody's business.

I picked one of our nicer local spots—a French-Thai place that was impossible to get into on the weekends but fairly empty during the week. It was lush, over-the-top decorated and overpriced. The kind of place Kayreen would like. I sat waiting for her, reading an old issue of *New York* magazine, conscious of the lilies in the gilded urn that sat near the maitre d's stand because the smell was so pungent. No sooner had I turned back to the article on doggie day care in Manhattan, when in breezed Kayreen in her magenta suit and bulky white and yellow-gold jewelry, hair pressed to her shoulders, Kelly bag in the fold of her arm, lipstick bright red.

"*Darlin'* Ina, how long has it *beean*?"

We air kissed each other as the maitre d' pulled out her seat and she sat down.

"So sorry I'm late. Girl, got the rich clients from hell, you hear me," she said, as she placed her napkin on her lap.

"I'm so happy you could meet me. I know how busy things are."

"Honey, I'm glad for the break, otherwise you just go, go, go, runnin' yourself crazy.

"Listen, I heard about you and Jay and honey, I was just . . . well, I don't know what to say. The two of you, well, you were just the cutest things. Nothing much surprises me, you know that, but that, *humph,* that one really knocked me *ovah.* I need a drink. You drinkin'?"

"Yeah, sure. I'll have a drink."

I'd weaned Ivy.

She held her finger up, like only a one-time debutante can, and ordered martinis for both of us.

"Now, what you wanna know, 'cause I know this isn't just a social call," Kayreen said, getting right to business as always. It was what I liked about her.

Our drinks came and we both took a big swallow. We each ordered the luncheon specials.

"Well, Kayreen, I don't know what I want, or I should say, why I want to know, but I'm just very curious about who this Julie Jarvis is and just what Jay is up to."

Kayreen held up her hands as if to say, *say no more.*

"Honey, I know, that's perfectly natural. You should've

seen me when Mel left me, trying to get any scrap of info I could about that slut. Of course, not being in the same social circles, well, there was no one I knew who knew her. It took quite a bit of tracking down, but I did . . ."

"Did it help? I mean, did you feel any better once you knew?"

"No I didn't, but at least I had some facts to chew on instead of what my imagination could come up with. That'll always make them seem better than they are."

"So do you know anything?"

Our crab and mushroom soups arrived and Kayreen took two spoonfuls and pronounced that it was *deevine*; Kayreen dotted the corners of her mouth with her napkin.

"Well, I know about her daddy—R. T. Jarvis; he was big in his day, sixties, seventies. He was in tight with the mayor of New York at the time, was it Beame or Lindsay? Anyway, he had all kinds of city contracts; more money than he could spend. Built a big ole house in Sag, had a twenty-room something on Hamilton Terrace, a jet, you know they were high cotton, no question. He and his wife, somebody Mama knows, she's from—I wanna say Nashville, but I'm not sure. Anyway, they had a girl and a boy, you know, typical gorgeous children—private school, Yale, all that. I don't think the boy turned out too well, married some hillbilly and is livin' somewhere in Maine or New Hampshire, one of those states where they got two black people. Anyway, Julie always has been something special. Pretty, smart, nice and of course, Daddy's girl . . ."

I cut in 'cause I didn't want to hear any more about the perfect Julie Jarvis, I just wanted the dirt.

"Kayreen . . ."

"I know, I know. You don't wanna hear all this; I'm just trying to think as I talk. Let's see, I know one thing, she's been out here like the rest of us . . . I know you've been married a while . . . but baby, let me tell you, you can't find a decent man, especially a black one, no—it ain't just the black ones. My white girlfriends can't find one, either. Anyhow, things ain't been no different for her, finding one that's got his own and wants to stick around for longer than a pig eats his slop."

"So she figured she'd just help herself to somebody else's," I snarled.

It came out as harsh as I intended.

Kayreen reached across the table to pat my hand.

"Baby, I know it hurts like hell. Believe me, I know."

Our salads came and mine remained untouched. Kayreen took a few bites and pushed hers aside.

"Is there anything I can do?" she asked.

"Yes, there is. You can find out what Jay intends to do. I haven't a clue and I can't get anything from him . . ."

"What makes you think he has any plans?"

"Well, the Jay I know always does."

"What are you thinkin', sweetheart?"

"I want to know if it's serious. I have to talk to the kids. If he's serious about her, thinking of marrying her."

"Well, I think that's probably what Julie has in mind. I mean, she must be in her thirties now and I'm sure Mama and Daddy ain't too happy with just havin' them half-hillbilly grandbabies, so she gone have to get on the stick . . ."

Suddenly it occurred to me that this lunch was a bad idea. I didn't need to know all this about the woman Jay had left me for, I didn't want to imagine him with another family while mine was discarded like some old White Castle cartons. The thought of my kids being shoehorned into somebody else's household made me feel lower than a pregnant snake—as Kayreen would say.

"Listen, if it's any consolation at all, let me just tell you that you'll get through this. I did and I'm better for it. I don't have a man, but so the hell what. I have my boys; you know the baby's down at Morehouse. I've got my work and my dogs and my friends, life does go on, baby girl."

Kayreen picked the chicken chunks out of her salad and continued.

"But some folks are still managing to find somebody to marry. I just went to two weddings, both forty-five-year-old black men gettin' married for the first time," Kayreen said, blotting her lips on a cocktail napkin.

"*Mmm-hmph,* both married other—Indian, Asian, Latino, whatever. One is fifteen years his junior, but hey, the niggas finally got married. Look, let's face it, they say we're just too much, too loud, too demanding, too in your face, too successful, too hardheaded. Mel ran off with a twenty-two-year-old blonde who couldn't spell it. I've got a master's in applied math. Go figure."

She reapplied her bright red lipstick.

"My brother Jimmy just left his wife of twenty years for a younger model—a Texas deb who collects diamonds. What're ya gonna do, Ina girl. What're ya gonna do?"

Chapter FOURTEEN

Before I married Jay, we'd stay up till three talking with people who had ideas and passions, who saw in the world some wonder and passion. Once I had children, I couldn't stay up past eleven o'clock and Jay seemed more interested in people he could make deals with, the social was always seen as a way to advance the professional, so I went along—pushing away any ennui I felt for the comfortable life we now all had and learned to make do with Paula Sweet's dinner parties.

Paula Sweet's house was a few blocks from ours. I knew her from the mommy group in Brooklyn Heights and now our children were in Ashley and Amir together. She did everything well. She cooked like a gourmet, she decorated like Bunny Williams, and she played tennis like she might be competing with Venus. Of course everyone has their warts, but anyway, she always invited us to her par-

ties and we always walked the few blocks away and in-
variably spent the walk home doin' postparty, which con-
sisted of Jay pointing out any new work they'd done. *Did
you see their workout room? They have more weights than
the Y,* or *Did you see the pavers in the driveway? That costs
a fortune.*

I'm standing at the buffet in the great room of Paula's
House Beautiful home. A $20,000 television (Jay told me
later) is pasted on the wall like a Jacob Lawrence. A pre-
fight gabfest is showing. There are things now that I suddenly don't get, like how a TV can cost this much and are
there really this many multimillionaires buying them. I'm
beginning to feel like Rip, like I've been asleep for an awfully long time and have woken up to a new world. In a
way, I am asleep. Put there by my own wish to check out
from a world that had gotten too fast and thin. I'd wanted a
quieter life; a child, a house, to do my photography when I
felt like it. For a while it seemed doable: mother, take pictures, go to dinner parties. Then I stopped taking pictures
and personal maintenance and shopping became my
hobby and I joined organizations for my children and they
took over my time, my brain went to sleep and then the social whirlpool sucked me under. But I don't know all this
yet.

The plate I'm holding is some exquisite pattern on porce-
lain so fine I forget I'm holding anything. The spread, always perfection, is Tuscan. It's her spring gathering, to
welcome a new couple into our fold. He is average-looking,

powerful and becoming rich; his wife, everything in place—casual and expensive, bejeweled with a tepid disposition. He listens in as I explain to a dinner patron the art program I'm working on for the Ashley and Amir black history program; he introduces himself, again, over aperitifs, where most of the men are in rapt attention of said television now broadcasting the fight. Jay loves these crowds of mostly business and law shakers and wannabes. He's in constant network mode, handing out cards, collecting them, talking loud and incessant. It exhausts me to watch him. It seems a form of relaxation for him.

"So what do people do around here for fun, I mean, other than the soccer games?" he says to me, breaking away from the fight herd. I'm struck by how he seems to listen to me. Not in a patronizing, overly interested way, but in a way that I know he is measuring every word I say.

"Fun," I repeated, laughing at the notion of such in a place like this. Not that our leafy community is lacking in merriment, but it's not the main draw. People move out here for their kids. Either because they had one too many and double or triple private school tuition would be prohibitive, or they gave up the vision of themselves as hip or creative or bohemian or sophisticated. He had come because his wife wanted to. He preferred the city and would continue to keep an apartment there.

"I guess most people still go into the city for that. Fun, I mean."

He looked at me and asked if I go in and if so, would I like to walk him through a photo gallery one day.

"You could help me. I know nothing about art or photography. Maybe we could go to that show, the one on lynching. Have you seen it?"

"No, I hadn't been able to bring myself to see it. But I am kind of curious about it."

I met him outside the International Center for Photography, where a small line has formed. He stepped out of the line when I got there, ushering me away by the elbow.

"You don't want to see this," he said.

"But . . ."

We walked out to Fifth Avenue and hailed a cab.

"The line's too long."

We stand facing each other as cabs whiz by.

"You hungry? I didn't eat," he said, as he reached for the cab's door.

"I could eat, but I thought you really wanted to see the show."

"I did see. I think you were right to follow your first instinct about it. You've seen the shit before and once is more than enough."

We ended up at a burger and beer joint on the Upper West Side, near the apartment he kept, and after a couple of dark beers we were both feeling easy and knew the exhibit had just been a ruse.

We ended up in the apartment he kept. "She's just so dumb, she's just so dumb." He said it over and over. He was talking about his wife during a postcoital cigarette. Neither of us smoked in our real life, but this was an altered existence. This was our moment away from paying bills, going to meetings, the laundry. This little thing was what was saving us from drowning under the drone of everydayness. He wasn't my usual type. He was on the large side, around six foot three, skin like a Mounds bar and arm muscles like mangos. Jay's opposite. He wore the close-cropped hair favored by black men of his age and status and had an average-looking face, not particularly handsome and not unattractive. He had something boiling under his smooth exterior, most of it anger that he'd never admit to, but I saw it as soon as we met and it was what drew him to me. He knew I saw him, saw beyond his credentials, saw him. No one had done that for a long time, maybe not since his high school basketball coach, who he considered responsible for all his subsequent academic and financial success. Now he found himself in a prison of his own making and it pissed him off. He, with all that brainpower, couldn't figure out how to get out of his box.

"It would cost me a fortune. She'd take my kids away. She's too dumb to raise them without me . . ." he'd lament at the thought of getting out of his marriage, which he saw as the primary source of his frustration.

"Why didn't I marry somebody like you," he said, reaching for the cigarette I held between my fingers.

"You wouldn't have liked me if we met before," I said, snuggling up to him under the fabulous scalloped-edged sheets.

He leaned over me and put the cigarette out in the glass ashtray. He kissed me on the shoulder and said, "I sure like you now."

"I'm on Prozac."

It was the wonderful thing about affairs—total truth and total bullshit rolled up together for both of you to know. He needed just what he got, a docile wife who was no threat to his intelligence and was pretty enough to make him look good, but not so beautiful as to be a distraction for him to always be wondering which man was hitting on her, lusting after her. He needed to marry, as he did, a woman whose background would help move him among people he wanted (he'd say needed) to move among. I didn't have any of that.

I'd noticed them out once, at the opera. He hadn't seen me. I watched her. She sat there, posture perfect, her hair slicked back and up into an oversize bun, makeup flawless, large South Sea pearl earrings and matching strand that, even wholesale, cost as much as a good used car. She wore a black sheath, sleeveless and just the right to-the-knee length. I was surprised she didn't wear opera gloves; this woman was so turned out, so perfect for the occasion. I let my mind wander over her, about her, imagine what her life was like outside this theater. Was she happy? Was she a good mother? A sexy wife? A taskmaster? From the looks of her, and we all know you can't judge a book by, well you know, but never mind that, she seemed stern, stern with herself. Look at her. Her laugh, with her husband's business associates, the ones who no doubt had invited them into their box, with its private party and expensive champagne. Who was this woman, I wanted to know. I wanted to listen to her conversation. Would she lie and say she enjoyed the performance or would she just comment on the beauty of the costumes and the set? She took her husband's arm as they walked the incline, out of the theater, her fuchsia satin wrap, dragging the floor ever so slightly. Was that for effect? It, too, was perfect in its imperfection. He looked striking in his custom tuxedo and pumps. He whispered something to her and she laughed and tossed her head back, just enough to let us know she thought him delicious. He was, in a kind of raw-boned, wide-mouth, broad-nose and strong-teeth way; she of delicate frame, high, prominent forehead and pointy nose and chin. Together they were a vision, a puzzle. She seemed mysterious, aloof, but she had just the kind of looks to procure a powerful man. But what did she think about? She had the behaviors down, the deference to him, the Nancy Reagan gaze, looking up at him, into his eyes as he uttered anything at all. Just the thing all those books on how to get a man, make a man fall in love with you tell you to do. Of course, I always wondered, what happened when you stopped pretending . . . what happened to the relationship? He couldn't love you anymore, because you weren't the you you said you were. He was free to leave. You were a fraud. Then there are those relationships where the people see each other—the good, the bad, the indifferent. What happens then? Are those inherently better? Letting it all hang out . . . this woman surely didn't. Nothing hung that wasn't supposed to, not a thread, a hair, a thought. What must it be like to be that tightly wound, that perfectly presented? What kind of prison? What kind of circumstance created this? Did she wear the clothes her mother laid out for her, or maybe her mother had been some hag who drank milk out of the carton? Or maybe it was the father; some militaristic iceman, maybe an Air Force lieutenant.

"I saw you one night. The two of you, at the arts center," I confess to him.

"You did? What did you see?"

"The interaction between you, it was quite a show."

"Oh yeah," he said, suddenly sounding self-conscious.

"She's quite pretty," I said, trying to make him feel better.

"That's her bonus added."

"Is she really vacant or is that just for you?"

He chuckled. I knew that it sounded cruel, but I didn't care. I hated her for pulling off what I couldn't—at least not without pharmaceutical aid. I wanted to be perfectly turned out, a sphinx, to be content with unlimited use of a platinum card. I rolled over so that I was pressing my crotch against his ample, muscled thigh. I didn't want to think about her or him or myself. I wanted to feel the juice from a ripe sweet plum run down my chin. That was how being with him felt. It was how I wanted my life to be, that succulent, to be that present all the time, to know that every moment is this precious, wondrous thing.

"She's actually quite educated," he said.

"Really?" I said, sarcastically, realizing I'd hit a nerve, the I-can-talk-about-my-mama-but-you-can't one.

"She went to Princeton."

"Of course." I didn't want to talk about this anymore. I didn't want to talk.

"But, of course, you know the difference between that and intelligence."

"Mmm," I said, now rubbing my cheek on his chest.

"You are intelligent, probably too much for your own good."

I moved my face lower. Finally he stopped talking.

Our thing lasted for a few months, until he decided that I was way too complicated or, as he'd said, heady for the kind of affair he wanted. A fling, a side dish, is supposed to be light and easy, he said, and I, even medicated, was never that.

FIFTEEN

J ay called two days before Christmas with a proposal. He wanted to spend the night on Christmas Eve so he could help with the toys and be there the next morning when the kids awoke. I reluctantly agreed. At least, I thought, I could put off another day having to tell the children what the deal was.

He arrived, as planned, with our usual Chinese takeout dinner. The tree was half-trimmed, the fire was going, Nat "King" Cole was on the CD player and all of our stockings in gold and silver, touches of red velvet, were hung and stuffed. The smell of fresh pine, cinnamon and orange floated in the air. Martha would've been proud. I made sure the kids were rested and well behaved and I even put a little effort into my appearance, exchanging my jeans for a wool jersey top and pants and a little extra makeup.

Jay came through the front door carrying bags of

wrapped gifts and a grease-stained brown bag and the boys went flying to him, jumping on him, yelling Daddy, Daddy, vying for hugs and kisses and attention. I stood back, holding Ivy on my hip, who was also reaching for Da-da. Tears came to my eyes and I quickly wiped before anyone noticed. I watched and waited. He came to me and kissed me warmly—on the cheek, saying something about how beautiful I looked. I took the shopping bag of food from him and told him we were starved and we all went into the kitchen. After we ate, the kids went to finish decorating the tree. I cleaned off the table, put the dishes in the dishwasher as Jay sat at the table playing with Ivy on his lap. He looked great. Better than I could ever remember. He looked stronger, more vibrant and he'd lost a little weight. He looked like he'd been pampered; his skin looked as if he'd been having facials, his haircut was better. I could just imagine her arranging all of it for him. Spending their free time shopping at Barneys, her standing behind him as he picked through a pile of cashmere sweaters, nodding her approval, frowning when she didn't and him blindly taking her counsel as Malcolm used to take mine.

Could he really have been that miserable with me, with us? Right now everything felt so normal, having all of us together on Christmas Eve. I wanted to enjoy it. I wanted to make him say he'd been a fool.

"You look nice," he said, as Ivy gnawed on his finger, drooling on his pin-striped pants.

I wiped down the granite countertops, thinking what a beautiful kitchen this was and heard myself acknowledge his compliment.

"Why don't you sit down for a minute?" he said, as if things were normal between us.

I realized I'd practically been in constant motion since he'd arrived.

I sat down, across from him at the farm table I must have spent six months searching for. It had to seat six, have just the right shade of brown chestnut and the right amount of nicks.

We looked at each other. I was aware that I hadn't seen him in almost three months. We'd never been apart for more than a few days in the almost fourteen years we'd been married.

"So how've you been?" he said.

I hunched my shoulders, as if to say, *how do you think*. I said, "Oh, fine."

"Really, Ina. I know this is tough. I feel terrible about it . . ."

"Well, Jay, you don't look it."

He looked down at Ivy's head, curled a finger in one of her ponytails.

"Looks like you found something you want more than us," I added.

My words smacked him hard.

"I deserved that," he said. "But it's not like you think. I mean the whole thing with . . . I mean, it's not about her."

"Oh no. So what is it about?"

"I don't know. I can't explain it. We were having problems for a long time. I just had to get out, or I was going to lose it."

"And what about me. You think doing the same thing

day in and out, dealing with three kids, basically on my own, is easy? Giving up my own dreams?"

"I never asked you to give up your dreams."

He sighed and said that he understood things hadn't been easy for me, but he just felt more and more pressure to just bring in the dough.

"There was just no fun. It was all just . . ."

"Drudgery?" I said.

"No Ina, it wasn't all drudgery," he said, as he put Ivy down so she could crawl to where her brothers were noisily putting ornaments on the tree.

"She's so pretty," he said, looking after her puffy backside swaying from side to side as she crawled out of the kitchen in her pink velour onesie.

I looked after her, too, and had to agree, but my smile was quickly replaced by the thought of what we were doing to her, to them.

"So do you want to marry this Julie person?"

It was the first time either of us had said her name. She was as real now as if she'd been standing there, in the kitchen between us.

He looked down, somewhere between his legs and repeated, softly, that this wasn't about her.

I felt heat rise up and go from my chin to the top of my head.

"I'm going to go put some sheets on the bed in the guest room," I said and left the room, stomping up the stairs like a thirteen-year-old.

I stayed upstairs for the rest of the night, torturing myself for not forcing Jay to tell me what he was doing, for missing the chance to have some semblance of family time. Jay bathed them, read the story and marched them each into my sitting room to say good night. I was on my chaise flipping through magazines. Malcolm forced me to look into his eyes where we each saw the well of sadness. I held his face between my hands and kissed both cheeks. I whispered, "Maybe Santa brought you that Xbox."

"Maah," he whined and smiled his half smile at me, his way of reminding me that he no longer believed in Santa Claus.

I read a little longer before nodding to sleep in the chaise, getting myself up to put on a nightgown and then into bed.

In the blackness of my bedroom, I came out of my deep fog sleep, awakened by Jay crawling into my bed, our bed, onto me. He put his mouth on mine and I greeted his tongue like the woman I was—starved. We kissed each other hard and fast and rubbed our bodies together as if we needed to, whispering each other's names over and over again . . . I want you. My cotton nightgown was wet through. He took his thickness from the opening in his boxer shorts and rubbed it against me. I felt myself rub onto him, so oozy, like sap from a maple. He moaned and so did I, and he put it inside me, knowing my body as he did, that I was ready. He pumped into me and I did the same, with him on top for a while and then me rolling onto him where I rocked my body until I came, sounding like some kind of predator, not caring if I woke up the kids, the neighbors, unaware of anything around me. He followed me and we collapsed into each other, lying sideways in our king-size bed. He kissed me on the mouth, a long tongue kiss, the kind we'd stopped doing long ago.

The next day I woke up to the smell of waffles and giggles coming from downstairs. I'd slept till nine. I looked around at the crumpled bed and was reminded of what happened last night. I resisted grabbing my robe for a moment to lay with my thoughts. We hadn't made love that way since we were first married. What had happened? Why had we stopped? Would it have made a difference if we hadn't? There were times in our marriage when I felt that I was in love with Jay, that I was happy I'd married him, when I didn't think I should've chosen David. We had grown closer as our family grew, as our attitudes grew up. I had begun to feel a settledness that wasn't settling for, but a simmering down, into a good heat just right for the stew we were making. It had taken a while before I actually felt married, probably five, six years. But now the biggest slap was that I'd finally gotten to where he was— where he'd wanted me to be—and then he up and left. That's the part that I couldn't process.

"God, Ma, it's about time," Marcus said as I entered the kitchen.

"Yeah, Ma, we've been waiting all this time to open the presents," Malcolm added.

"I'm so sorry, I know how hard it is to wait . . ."

Ivy was happily gnawing a teething biscuit, sitting in her high chair.

"I let them each open one," Jay said.

"Good, now go, start opening the rest, I just need to get some coffee," I said. They ran into the living room.

Jay came up behind me at the stove, hugging me around the waist and kissed me on the neck.

"Thanks for last night."

I felt shy and didn't want to acknowledge what had happened or deal with the questions of what next.

"Okay, kids, let's see what you got," he said, clapping his hands together, leaving the kitchen to join them.

I was feeling good and confused and happy and I don't know what. Does this mean he's coming back or was it just a fuck? I sipped my coffee and followed him into the living room. At the moment I didn't care.

The day went on like every other Christmas we'd had in the past with the kids playing with their toys, the TV blaring college football and the phone ringing with relatives and friends calling in to say merry Christmas. Jay's mother spent alternate holidays with us and with his brother's family in the Poconos. This was her year with them in Pennsylvania. My parents were coming later for an early dinner. It was almost two in the afternoon before I even got dressed. I just wanted to freeze this moment, this day. Well, it was over soon enough when the doorbell rang. I looked at Jay, who looked like he might've seen a ghost. It was early for my parents to show up.

"I'll get it," Jay said, getting up from the sofa.

The kids were still preoccupied with all their booty; Ivy was napping in her playpen.

My eyes followed Jay to the door, where I could see a woman's hair and part of a fur coat. He was speaking so low I couldn't begin to hear him. I asked who it was and when I didn't get an answer, my heart froze. Jay closed the door on the woman and told me he'd be right back. He reached for the hall coat rack, grabbed his blazer and went out of the house. I ran to the window and saw him with a woman getting into a dark sedan, one of those company call-cars that transport professionals in and out of the city. It hit me like a Chicago winter wind that it was Julie Jarvis.

I moved passed pissed into some other world of hormone-induced emotion that I was sure I'd never before felt. It was something primal. I felt high, not that burning anger. I was the mother mammal in the woods who'd been left alone, abandoned by her mate, who seemed to finally find his way back to our perch, cave, nest—home. Now the interloper had come onto my territory, my nest, to get him. I didn't bother putting on anything. I knew I wouldn't feel the cold. I felt my slippers unsteady on the icy walk and remembered that I hadn't put out any sand, which was another Jay chore that I'd forgotten to pick up. I held on to the wrought-iron banister and gingerly headed toward the car parked in our circular drive toward the right of the house. I got to the car and pounded on the darkened window. I heard the power bring the back window down and my face was practically touching Jay's, who was trying his hardest to remain calm. She looked startled and scared and I could tell she'd been crying.

"What the *fuck* are you doing coming to my house," I said, ignoring Jay, who was now trying to get out of the car. I snatched open the front door and got in. The two of them had been sitting in the center of the backseat. The driver had abandoned his car and was on the front lawn smoking, probably thinking, I've seen it all now. I leaned over the seat, now pointing my finger at her; she was braced against the back, looking like she was trying to keep from being eaten by the lioness now facing her.

"I asked you a question. What the fuck are you doing at my house? On Christmas day, where my children live, looking for my goddamn husband? What kind of slut are you? Could you be any more desperate? Did you grow up in a fucking barn?"

"Okay Ina, that's enough," Jay said, in his deep I'm-in-control voice.

"Shut up," I said. "I wanna hear from your girlfriend here."

Julie looked down into the wad of tissues she had in her hands. Another tear, making her nose red.

"Look, I didn't mean to upset you," she finally said.

"I'm *way* fuckin' past upset . . ."

"Look, I see this was a bad idea. I just didn't know what else to do, today just brought down all this stuff and I guess the reality of this situation. I guess I just needed to see it all to make it be real to me . . ."

"So until now we were all phantoms? Well, guess what—there are three very real children inside that house, and there are years inside that house you're look-ing at. I don't know what Jay told you and I really don't give a shit right now. I can see he's obviously made you feel it was okay to pull some shit like this and show up here today . . ."

"Wait a minute, Ina—" Jay tried to interrupt and I kept talking like he hadn't said anything.

"I'm his wife and their mother and we were living as we were, a family, and then one day he tells me he's leaving, doesn't mention anything about you. I have to find out about you in the newspaper. Did you know that? The last three months have been hell, but . . . Jay clearly doesn't know which end is up, or he does and he's too chicken to tell one of us . . ."

"Is that true, Jay?" she said, sounding stronger.

Now Jay looked away, out the window, his thumb and pointer finger holding up his face.

He was silent; guess he figured the less said the better.

"Are you going to answer her?" I said, now leaning across the seat, ready to pimp-slap him.

He cut his eyes at me and said he just needed some time.

"Time?" we both screamed.

"Look, Ina, you need to go back into the house, and Julie, you should go back to New York. This is not—"

"And who appointed you judge? I'm not going any-where until you tell your girlfriend here what your plans are. Why don't you tell her about last night."

He now put his head down, as if to say, *no, she didn't go there.* He'd clearly underestimated the situation and how desperate I felt. I'd say or do anything at this point. I had nothing more to lose.

"What happened last night, Jay?" she asked like a lawyer cross-examining, knowing the answer.

"Ina, would you please go inside. I'll be in shortly."

"No."

With my answer pushing him into what he must have decided was an untenable position, he got out; Julie called after him and then she got out. He turned and they talked facing each other, standing in the driveway. I looked toward the house and saw my worst fear realized—two heads at the window watching.

"Good going, Jay," I said, as I passed them on my way back inside.

Jay took a quick look for himself before turning to Julie to say good-bye, leaving her crying in front of our house.

Bring On the Pain

PART II

SIXTEEN

When my grandmother left my grandfather she had two young children, Aunt Juneann and Aunt Rayleen, and was pregnant with my mother. My grandmother left my grandfather down south because he used to beat her, sometimes with logs they used to heat their home. She left for an unknown life in Pomona, knowing only that it had to be better than the dusty southern life she'd fled. They settled in the small, quaint town settled by Puritans and the Dutch that had a reputation for tolerance. A northern city, fifteen miles from New York City, where there had been a community of *Negroes* as far back as the 1800s, so seeing dark faces was no big deal. It appealed to my grandmother's sense of who they were, a place where they could be themselves— noble, working-class—and not be stifled by prejudice and small mindedness. A place where Grandmother would comfortably walk around in her snood and with her corn pipe; Aunt Juneann could always be overdressed in frilliness; Rayleen, who grew to nearly six feet, could feel superior to everyone and my mama could become an artist.

While the freer North was generally good for the Eleazers, for Rayleen it brought out all her ways and at sixteen she was sent away to the Annie Boroughs School for Girls, a jail-like house in Newark where the *crime* most committed was getting pregnant without benefit of a marriage license. Aunt Rayleen gave birth to Paris, my cousin, who Aunt Juneann raised as her own. Aunt Rayleen could've done what people did at that time—got married in Grandma's parlor—but she refused, said she simply wasn't interested in any of kind of life that had been planned for her. She didn't want to get married and drink tea and belong to the Pomona Women for Progress. Rayleen liked men and plenty liked her. She liked their company, the tobacco smell mixed with bergamot, but she liked to live alone, to be with her own thoughts without having somebody saying, "Penny for your thoughts" or "What's on your mind, sunshine?" Those comments irritated the hell out of Rayleen and sometimes wiped away all the good stuff that had come before. She'd had lots of men, more than a lady was supposed to, but she thought it was her right. Years later, when she ended up bleeding to death on a cold bathroom floor, all of us Eleazer women mourned the filly in all of us, in all women who'd been cut short because they wanted to be free.

After my mama saw what defying her mother got Aunt Rayleen, she decided she'd play the game, do what her mother wanted her to do, wear the clothes that were laid out for her.

The house my grandmother used to live in was a little bigger than my room, she tells me one night after her eyes got too tired reading my books and she began to tell me stories about growing up down south, about how she'd had to walk to school, five miles there and five miles back, and how she never owned her own shoes—she and her five sisters would share them. She still has the corns to show for it. But her mother, my great-grandmother, didn't care what Grandma had to go through to get to school. "You gone be knowin' someum and that's all there's is to it."

Grandma, like many Eleazers before her, was a contradiction: a down-home, elegant woman. My grandmother was the type to show up at a memorial service in a limo with two homemade hams wrapped in aluminum foil. A walk and a look that says, *I define my own fabulousness.* It never seemed a struggle for her. She just accepted who she was and didn't spend any time trying to convince others. I think my mom was always trying to rectify what was inside with what the world saw, and oftentimes her laboratory was me. Ultimately she'd check out altogether rather than figure out how to make peace with all that she was that didn't seem to make sense to most folks.

Down in Little Mountain, where our family worked a three-hundred-acre plantation, from can't see to can't see for nothing and endured; they nursed white babies while their own were taken from them and sold; saw husbands strung up till the little bit of life they had was choked out, these women held on, putting little bits of gold away, saving up, determined to buy their way out of the horror in which they lived. Freed between their own efforts and, finally, the legal end to slavery, the family remained in Little Mountain. They stayed on the plantation, sharecropping until Great-aunt Sophia ended up beaten close to death for being true to herself, trying to hold onto a Hershey's kiss worth of Eleazer dignity. When she said *I don't clean nobody's house but my own,* the white woman who was asking, or more accurately, telling Sophia that she would clean, Sophia told the woman furthermore to kiss her ass. Her reaction caused a riot of white folks walking round like rabbits straight outta Alice's Wonderland, with Sophia standing center stage, defiant, too much for South Carolina near the turn of the century. Four white men grabbed Sophia by her extremities and hauled her, like they mighta been carrying a tree trunk, off to a place where they'd take us to remind us of our place.

No-good bitch, animal, heifer, trifling, dirty, nasty, sex-crazed. Southern whites felt free to hurl such words at black women. But who's the animal? Who's inhuman?

The Eleazer women always understood that who they were didn't begin and end with being property. They knew in their bones that they were descended from people who owned themselves, possessed humanity, intelligence and ability. That spirit was what propelled Grandma out of there with two babies in tow and one growing inside her. That spirit was in me.

SEVENTEEEN

Zackie was getting his GED at the night school downtown. I was on my way home when I bumped into him at the bus stop. The last real conversation we'd had was when Aunt Rayleen died and that had been a few years ago now.

"Hey girl," he said. We kissed on the cheek, each leaving a mark; mine was a Mary Quant clear lip gloss, his Flori Roberts deep burgundy stain.

His Afro wig had been replaced by a short straight pageboy. He wore dark jeans and a shirt tied at the waist, high-heeled clogs and a large patchwork leather purse.

"You look good," I said and meant it.

"Thank you, girl. You look . . ." he paused, checking me out in my matching pink-and-white gingham outfit. "Sweet."

I knew all about the family drama that had Uncle Ben chasing Zackie down Chancellor Avenue, catching him and hitting him so hard his wig came off and a molar was knocked loose.

"Where are you living? Everybody's afraid to mention your name, especially if Uncle Ben is around."

"You seen my dad?"

"Not recently."

"Oh girl, it's just been so much drama just to see Juneann, I can only see her at cousin Paris's. Daddy 'bout had a heart attack when he saw me in full drag, honey, tried to do a Sonny Corleone on me. Pulled that Caddy over and jumped out—ee-oh girl, it was too much."

I didn't know what to say, although I knew the sighting had just been too much for Uncle Ben.

I sighed, feeling sorry for both of them. I knew his father believed, as Christians believe in Jesus, as Muslims believe in Allah, that he couldn't let his son walk through the streets dressed like a woman.

"Gave me a black eye, chil'. That thing took months to heal."

I wanted to hug him, but knew that his shell had hardened to a point that had made our old childlike relationship almost obsolete.

"But at least everything's out in the open now, as much as old Ben can't stand it. I'm free." He said the last part shaking his head dramatically, side to side, a little of the wig flopping onto his forehead. He howled at his emancipation. I missed him and was repelled by him.

"So what have you been up to, Miss Girl?"

"Well, I'm looking at colleges now. I think I've narrowed down my choices . . ."

"That's great. We have to get together so you can tell me all about it. My bus is coming. Call me at Paris's."

He air kissed me good-bye and shook his wrist for the bus to stop.

I stood there, feeling embarrassed as I watched him get on the bus, full of attitude, his preemptive dis armor against the disapproving looks from the bus driver and passengers. His behind settled in the jeans, his slightly slew-footed strut were exactly as Aunt Juneann's. He even held his head high like a Yorkie sniffing the air, just like his mother, too. He took a seat by the window and waved and held his knuckles on his cheek, with his pinkie and thumb sticking out.

I nodded okay, but knew I wouldn't call. I knew he knew that, too. It was just easier for both of us to keep the space between us, to pretend we'd chosen our way of being, to ignore what we meant to each other.

My mother insisted on having a graduation/going away to college party for me. She also invited every friend I'd had since I was a toddler: Darren, the girls from down south, Michelle and Stacey from public school along with the white girls from my time in private school. Uncle Ben refused to come when he found out Zackie was coming. The party was held in our recently renovated basement— knotty pine walls, bar with mirrored panels with gold veins throughout, red leatherette stools and plaid sofa. The hi-fi had an eight-track player and my dad stocked it with sound tracks from all-black movies from the seventies—lots of Isaac Hayes. He was the only one moving. To one side on a line of folding chairs were my friends from the public school, mostly black, and on the other, the mostly white ones, from Stone Ridge Country Day of the Scared Heart. I sort of stood in the middle, kind of like a talk show host, trying to get them to interact with each other, pointing out different things they had in common. Zackie came late and brought one of the guys from high school that he hung out with in the Village who acted like a girl, but didn't dress like one. I was mortified and hated myself for it. Zackie didn't wear a wig, but had on eyeliner and a purse slung across his torso.

I saw his platforms coming down the basement steps and heard him before his face was shown.

"Congratulations, girl!"

I felt my stomach tighten as my cheerleader friends shifted in their seats to get a look at the person who matched the voice.

He came to me and we hugged. Mine wasn't enthusiastic so he stepped back to look me in the face. His expression said, *oh, I see,* but he said nothing.

"Your mother told Juneann that you got into one of the fancy black schools and I wasn't a bit surprised, you know that."

I wanted to tell him that I loved him, but couldn't, didn't.

"Where's the punch," he asked, not acknowledging anyone else in the room. He did a quick check to see if the parents were around, then he pulled a brown paper bag from his large purse and emptied half of his Bacardi fifth into the Hawaiian Punch. He poured a Dixie cup for himself and his friend Roger.

"Now the party may commence."

He and Roger toasted their cups.

Darren, who did his high school years at an all-boys' Catholic school and was on his way to Morehouse, made his way to Zackie.

Zackie was standing with his back to Darren, drinking and talking with Roger.

"Hey Zackie, how you doin'?" Darren said, tentatively.

Zackie turned around dramatically, fixed Darren with an up and down stare.

"How'ma doin'? Well, look at me," he said turning his head in profile. "How do I look?"

Darren looked down at his black church shoes and stuck his hands in his pockets. Zackie, always the most sensitive person in the room, often pretended the opposite.

"How are *you* doing, Darren? You look well. Headed to Atlanta?"

Darren looked up at Zackie and smiled. He remembered his old friend and knew that he'd been spared one of his famous wolf tickets, a comment that could singe your clothes.

"Yeah, going to the House, math major."

"So you stayed with the numbers, huh?" Zackie said, turning to Roger. "Boy was almost as smart as me."

We all laughed, a slightly nervous one, the kind people do when the truth is shown with a magnifying glass.

"So what are you going to be? An accountant? A math teacher?" He rolled his eyes but stopped himself from saying what he was thinking, which was *how droll.*

Darren was considering accounting, but didn't want to risk seeming like a bore to Zackie. No one ever wanted to do that, so he just said he hadn't decided yet what he would do.

The newer friends just sat there talking to each other, stealing glances at Zackie. I wanted to kill my mother for inviting all these different pieces of me. I hadn't learned to put them all together, even that they did all fit, were each a part of me. Right then, I just wanted to find a hole and crawl in. Instead I drank punch.

My dad finally caught on that no one was dancing and put on a current record, "Shame." Everyone let out a *woo* or a grunt or a *that's my song,* chairs were pushed against the wall and platforms got to working onto the newly laid indoor/outdoor carpet.

Darren grabbed Cybil. The captain of the squad and Zackie and Roger started to penguin with me in the middle.

The punch was working.

"So these are your friends, huh?" Roger asked.

I nodded without passion.

"I remember these hos from high school. They were some stuck-up bitches, excuse me for saying so, but it's true. Wouldn't speak to nobody they didn't think was worth something."

"That's enough, Miss Roger," Zackie said. "I think she's had too much punch," he said to me.

"Honey, I ain't hardly drunk, but you know I got to call it like I see it," Roger said before taking a spin.

"Remember your company manners," Zackie said, dropping down into a low penguin. "*She's* just jealous they wouldn't let *her* become a cheerleader."

"I just think your cousin here seems like she's in a different league, that's all I'm sayin'."

Zackie looked at me, his liquid eyeliner making his eyes look even more exotic. "I've been telling her that all her life." Then he pretended to whisper, "But she *is* jealous of your friends."

The record was over and everybody was fanning with their hands and going for more punch.

"Where's the food? I know Aunt Leaver is up there throwin' down." He looked around.

"Honey, we gonna have to eat and run."

My mother and Aunt Juneann came downstairs, Aunt Juneann wearing her lace-trimmed holiday apron, and pushed their way to the buffet table carrying huge aluminum pans of macaroni and potato salad, colslaw, greens, burgers, hot dogs and, of course, fried chicken.

"Hey Aunt Leaver," Zackie said as my mother set the food down on the table.

"Zackie, is that you, darlin'?" She opened her arms and he walked into them. They hugged and swayed like the long-lost friends they were. I felt tears well up. Why couldn't I do that? I watched him introduce my mom and his mom to Roger. Mom and Aunt Juneann shook Roger's hand graciously and introduced him to my dad, who'd come out of his makeshift DJ booth in the back of the basement. True to his word they were ready to leave after they put down a couple plates of food.

"Walk us out, Miss Booty Face," Zackie said to me. He kissed his mother on the cheek, yelled good night to the room and I followed them up the stairs to the front of my house. He'd written his number on an index card and folded it up.

"Here's the number of a friend who always knows how to find me. If you ever need me, you better call, you hear?"

Tears rolled down my face and I didn't try to wipe them away.

"I love you," I finally blurted out.

Zackie put his hands on my shoulders and looked down at me. He was well over six feet barefoot and with Candies on he towered.

"I know that, and I love you back. You leave all this shit here, you hear? You go down to that college and let the girl I know back out," he said, pointing his finger into my chest.

CHAPTER

EIGHTEEN

I went to college determined to not fall into a group, a clique or one idea of how to be. I was going to live as Zackie told me—as my free self. I wouldn't try to be trendy; for one it was too expensive, and secondly it was limiting. It was much more fun going to thrift shops to put together my own look. I believed in wearing my hair natural and lived in the same jeans and clogs, which was a statement around all those folks, many of whom straightened their hair and wore pantyhose and pumps. With my bushy hair either out wild or wrapped under a bandanna, I was out of consideration for most of their clubs, which made my life easier. I had David and Leelah and that was enough. I knew somehow that I needed time to find that person Zackie was so convinced was there.

I got a job taking pictures for the campus weekly. I did it reluctantly, after Leelah began secretly dropping off my pictures. It was hard work, but fun and I learned a lot about what makes a good picture and all about the campus, which I would've never learned otherwise. I knew most of the deans, the academic affairs head, got real chummy with the head of student affairs—an extrovert who rolled around campus in a tweed jacket and a rose-colored silk scarf long enough to give Isadora Duncan pause. He reminded me so much of Zackie, who I still thought of often and always asked my mother about. Aunt Juneann would only tell me that he was living somewhere in Manhattan and doing fine.

When I came home for Christmas break I unfolded the index card he'd given me, but when that person didn't know where Zackie was I went next door to see Aunt Juneann with the intention of getting Zackie's number. He didn't call her, she said, as she quickly scrawled his number on a piece of paper bag and shoved it into my palm. She'd whispered to me as she walked me out of the house that the number was to a hall phone that I could try. I called the number as soon as I got home. Couldn't wait to tell him all about my years at school and going to the Caribbean with Leelah and her family and the hotel that looked like a mansion and had servants and a beach that only they used. I'd worked at a photography gallery and met fabulous people who all seemed to be living outside of the box. He would be so happy to hear I'd left behind normal and my drive to fit into something that I wasn't meant to. My thoughts were running so fast that I didn't realize that someone had answered the phone. I asked for Zackie and the person said "hole on" and dropped the phone.

The noise it made hitting the wall made me imagine a dank place with gray institutional walls and a faint whiff of piss. After what seemed like ten minutes Zackie got on the phone.

His voice was hoarse and his tone was scary.

"Zackie? Is that you? It's Ina."

"Ina? Ina Paris? No way. Gurl."

"I know it's been too long. How are you?"

He was silent for a second and I knew he was taking a drag from a cigarette.

"I been better and I probably been worse," he said, clearing his throat.

"Where are you living now, your mom didn't seem to know exactly where."

"Next to hell, but I'm in Manhattan. Just need to be making a few more dollars before I can move to Park Avenue, you know what I'm sayin'."

He laughed exuberantly.

I wanted to know so much, but didn't want Zackie to feel like I was prying.

"It would be great to see you while I'm home, you know, during the holidays."

"You can come here, if you like. I don't go there, you know, I'm not welcomed by dear old Daddy."

Aunt Juneann had to sneak to call him and see him. She had to pretend to not know where he was when I talked to her for fear of her husband overhearing her.

"How about if we meet someplace, in Manhattan? Maybe tomorrow?" I said.

He thought about it a minute and said sure. "I'll meet

you at Tad's on Thirty-fourth Street near Eighth. You re-member it?"

I smiled at the thought of that dive. It was a greasy diner fixed up with tablecloths to look like a real restau-rant and the first place Zackie and I went together on our preteen excursions into New York.

"I'll see you there tomorrow, about one?"

"Tomorrow. Ciao, baby."

The hawk whirled around the avenue as I waited on the bus. My down jacket was holding up fine in this weather, but I'd worn Frye boots instead of my usual waterproof hiking boots and my feet were damp. I didn't want to look like a total hayseed. My hair, which I normally wore in a full bush that circled my head like a large unshaped cloud, I'd today parted in the middle and braided two cornrows on each side. My skin was still recovering from it's acne phase, so I didn't bother it with makeup, just put on a little dark red lipstick.

I got to Tad's a little after one and was surprised to see Zackie sitting at a table, sipping a Coke and smoking a cigarette. He got up when he saw me, waving frantically at me until I ran to him and we hugged tight. He held me away by the shoulders and said, "Just let me look at you. You're grown! You look fabulous. Look at the hair . . ."

I cut him off, explaining in a breathless way that this wasn't the normal way I wore it . . .

"It's usually out, kind of like Chaka Khan, but . . ."

"Oh, it's fierce the natural way. Girrrl, I'm just loving it. This sorta preppy thing you have going. Girl, you're fierce."

I sat down to bask in Zackie's words, wishing I could somehow inhale them so that they would become a part of my insides. That I'd truly *feel* fabulous. I just nodded and said thanks. Zackie didn't look that great. He wore foundation, which clumped around his after-five shadow. He was growing out a perm, which he'd just slicked back and tied a bandanna on the back. He'd gained a little weight, but said he was happy 'cause he had been really thin just a few months ago.

"So tell me all about college life. You hungry? Order whatever you want. I just got paid."

We both ordered burgers and fries.

"You have a job?"

He took a sip of his Coke and looked at me with eyes wide.

"Of course, Miss Girl. I haven't found anybody to pay my bills . . . yet."

We laughed the way we used to.

"I'm a makeup artist."

Wow, I said, but what I thought was, What the hell is that? As usual, he read my mind.

"I put makeup on people, women, at Macy's and try to get them to buy as much as possible. Don't ever buy all the stuff, you hear me. I'll send you whatever you need."

I nodded dutifully.

"That's a nice color you're wearing. Who's that by?"

"I bought this lipstick at the drugstore."

I expected that admission to be met with one of his world-famous eye-rolling lectures of how uncool my purchasing habits were.

"Brava. That's my girl. The cheap shit's always better."

"Really?" I was incredulous.

After our lunch we sat and talked about school, I told him all about David and Leelah and how I'd never felt so free and how there wasn't that tension in college the way it was in high school where you had to choose to either ignore your white friends and sit at the cafeteria table with other black students or vice versa. I was talking so fast, I kept losing my breath, so excited to be in a place where race had finally become insignificant.

"Ain't got nothin' to prove," Zackie said, knowing just what I was talking about.

I felt so happy to again be there with my best cousin, my oldest friend, the one person who knew all about me and loved me anyway. Zackie just got it. He was born knowing and I felt lucky just to have him in my life again, even just for lunch.

"Why don't you come visit me? You ever been to D.C.?"

Zackie took a gulp of ice from his glass of Coke and began to chew it. He looked at me as if I were someone to be pitied. He shook his head no: "I don't think the good folks at Howard are quite ready for the likes of *moi*."

"But . . ." I said, stopping myself, deciding to change the subject.

He was determined to get to a better-paying job, maybe work at Bloomingdale's, get a nicer apartment and meet a man he could love, who would love him.

"It's hard to meet somebody decent in the clubs."

At the end of the afternoon I was sorry to have to get the

bus back home. I'd be leaving for D.C. in two days and wouldn't get to see Zackie again for a while.

The winter air had turned harsh and the walk to the Port Authority felt longer than it was. A prostitute propositioned me—did I look like a boy? Fortunately the bus was there and the ride home was only a half hour. No traffic.

CHAPTER NINETEEN

Sometimes the loneliness is so intense I have to laugh. It's the only way to bear it, but in a way it is funny, funny to seem so together, so fabulous on the outside, such an insider, so in the know, on the list, an "it" person and be so totally not that way inside. Inside I was just the strange little girl who my grandmother used to take to church with her 'cause my mother didn't believe in orga- nized religion. My grandmother thought I'd grow up cursed if I didn't at least know the Lord's Prayer. I would dress my- self in a tutu over jeans and yellow rubber boots with a peace symbol tie-dyed shirt and a tiara. For church—an old-fashioned black church. They'd whisper, *That's her grandbaby, yeah, Leaver's child. She's a little different. Well, so is that Leaver, don't you remember what she used to be like and look at her now, always in the paper for some kind of foolishness. Teaching kids somebody black invented the traf-*

fic light, what difference that gone make to these badass kids? Seems to me she just wasting her time. I just don't understand that Leaver, and you know Caledonia tried to do everything right for that girl. Guess she just trying to do the right thing by her grandbaby. That's all you can do.

My mother didn't believe in going to church, she thought it was just another prison. Of course, that kind of talk caused my grandmother to clutch her heart to keep it from cracking into tiny pieces. She knew God personally. How could her daughter blaspheme? My mother was teaching art to kids in government-sponsored community centers after school and in the summers. Not unlike David's mother, who had a law degree and a national platform. My mother used her art as a weapon and a shield.

"You scrubbed floors for me to go to college to get my degree, because I thought you'd want me to use my education, my freedom to help someone else. I didn't think you did all that for me to be driving a Mercedes-Benz," my mother would say to her mother whenever she complained about her community teaching. That's how I ended up going to church with Grandma.

My cousin Paris is a decade older than me. She has an undergraduate degree in biology, a master's in social work and part of a Ph.D. in American studies. She runs the counseling department at a battered women's shelter. She doesn't make any money, but doesn't care about material things. Her clothes are from places where she buys detergent in bulk or from the back of Ma's or Aunt Juneann's or my closet. Mama approves of her choices; admires her, which means she didn't approve of me when I became a suburban matron. Paris just had something that came from inside and she had perfect bones, features, head and body. It would be easy to be jealous of her if she wasn't so unaware of her looks.

"She looks like me," Ma would say if anyone complimented Paris in Ma's presence. It would be one of those moments when other people would get a glimpse of just how crazy Ma was. Both were beautiful but had very different looks. Paris was fine boned. Ma had a full face with rounded features. I was somewhere in between the two. I was lighter than Ma, darker than Paris. I have full, thick hair that curls if you don't comb it. Paris shaved hers off and Ma wears a curly wig. This wig wearing was an early sign that she was going down. She'd always had thick beautiful hair that was her pride. She'd spend hours on her hair, doing a light press, rolling it, combing it and talking about it. She swore that's why all the Eleazer women always had men—cause we all had a lotta hair, she'd say to anybody unfortunate enough to comment on hers. They would get an earful of the family saga; from Great-grandma Ina and Great-aunt Sophia in Little Mountain and the way those white men beat her. Maybe Ma was always a little bit crazy.

My mother was named Leaver after the first sign, an advertisement for soap, my grandmother saw when they crossed the Mason-Dixon and could move out of the segregated part of the train—the hottest part with the most uncomfortable seats. It was to be a symbol of freedom.

*   *   *

When I was growing up Mama would just disappear. Sometimes just overnight, sometimes for weeks before her emotions overtook her and she had to go somewhere and just lay down. That's the way she described it to me: "Sweetie, I just need to go somewhere and lay down." *Lay her heart down,* was what Grandma would have called it. Much later I would find out that Mama had friends and a life that had nothing to do with Daddy or me. Her friends were artists and musicians who drank and smoked pot and slept in the day and worked or partied at night. She used to take marathon sketching classes in New York, where models would stand—really they were just people, students, whatever, who needed money and had interesting bodies—would just stand and the artists would sketch for hours. They could stay all day and into the night or leave after an hour. I kept some of her sketchpads. She had had a gift but it was one she didn't know where to put. How many Negro women artists had you heard of in the fifties?

Outta the Box

PART III

CHAPTER TWENTY

I fall asleep and dream of Zackie. We're children and the wind is blowing our outfits that we've made of sheets. We have angel wings that billow and we're holding hands, playing some form of ring-around-the-rosy. We're children, but not small. We're so happy that our hearts pound, our faces hurt from smiling. The pure blue of the sky hurts, too. Looking at it, I feel God's grace. A few seconds later and the shade changes, ever so subtle, a lessening.

I wake up from having fallen asleep in the chair next to Zackie's hospital bed, where he is lying, elevated to make his breathing less labored. The nurse has come in to change his egg-crate foam padding—he lays on this to prevent bedsores, she's told me. I watch him carefully now. His body shrunken like a concentration camp survivor, only he won't survive this. My beloved Zackie is dying and it's coming soon, maybe this week the doctors say. His brain stopped functioning several days ago. These are our last moments together—I know I will hold them in my heart my whole life.

I replay, already, his last lucid words. He'd stretched out his arm for me to hold his hand. He'd looked at me and squeezed it.

"Don't be sad for me. I'm happy, Ina. Happier than I've ever been."

"How can that be?"

" 'Cause now I know. I know what life is supposed to be about. Things fall apart and get put back together, whether we do it or not, things get back together and then fall apart again. That's life, Ina."

He smiled and lit up my world.

"That's it, huh?" I'd said, trying to sound casual, trying to keep it light, to hide the feeling that my chest was breaking apart.

"I'm telling you this, this is my gift to you so that you'll live your life and stop being afraid and burdened. Things work out. You just need to be conscious. Don't go to sleep, don't play dead. Pay attention and feel, feel all of it, the good and the bad, 'cause the pain is where the lessons are."

We could be back on my front porch and he was talking, I'm seven, he's eight or we're sixteen and seventeen, catching snippets of what he's saying, but this time I'm comprehending more than just pieces.

"Don't try to avoid pain by shopping and dinner-partying and obsessing about your looks." His words came at me like a laser. I let myself feel the ache in my chest.

Tears ran as if a faucet had been turned on inside my head and forgotten about. I heaved and cried and wiped my face with the edge of my sleeve. I'd been given permission and I was grateful to let out all that I'd been holding onto for so long. I cried and Zackie lay there calm as a stone, looking at the ceiling, a tiny smile on his lips.

His hair is a little newborn patch, straight, covering only part of his head. He looks like he did when we were very little, three, four and I just can't help how much I love him.

"I need you," I whisper to him, sucking saliva back, clenching my back teeth shut.

"Please don't go. Don't leave me." He squeezes my hand again.

"You're the only one who knows me. Who knows all my secrets, who loves me anyway."

He just kept smiling his tiny smile, limply squeezing my hand, but not responding.

My life had moved along without Jay. I was so busy just trying to keep things floating, working two part-time jobs, shuttling the boys, leaving Ivy at Paige's when I had to go to work and my dad was too busy dealing with my mother's tenuous grip on sanity. The only time I had to think was the time I sat in the fake leather recliner watching Zackie die.

During one of our early hospital conversations I'd confessed to him that I was secretly relieved that Jay had left because it forced me to figure out what I wanted, how I wanted to live and I didn't have to endure any more client dinners or corporate trips or any filler that had made up our lives.

"Give Jay a chance. He does love you, let him see you," Zackie had said.

I couldn't believe what I was hearing and I told myself Zackie was merely delirious from all the medication. He had never thought Jay was right for me, he'd even said so, in so many words.

"I know what I said before, I didn't know anything. I was just talking. Jealous," he'd said.

"What're you talking about? You think, now, Jay is the one?"

"I think you should try to make it work, with your real self this time."

"Little point of order, Miss Thing; Jay left me, remember?"

"He left the person you were pretending to be, not you, not the real you, the one I know. The one he married."

I'd sat there rubbing my forehead, which was hot now from sitting in front of the sunny window. Zackie's eyes remained half-open. The machines were hissing and I sat back in the recliner, knowing I had to get on with preparing myself for what was coming, but how does one ever prepare?

Ever since the Julie Jarvis holiday arrival, Jay has been eating shit. When I announced that I didn't have the energy to throw a party for Ivy's first birthday after six months of raising the children alone, he said he'd do the whole thing: send invitations, get the entertainment, food, decorate, and make the goody bags, everything. Now this was to be a first, and only because I was so worn down did I let him. I secretly believed he'd fall on his face and everyone would see what a fuckup he is and appreciate me, the superior one who has been effortlessly organizing birthday parties and everything else about our lives for the last fourteen years. He also needed to make things right with the boys, who had refused to go with him to their annual holiday show and dinner.

During Christmas break, a few days after the Julie scene, I was helping the boys get dressed in their usual blazers, bow ties and blue oxford cloth shirts. They announced they didn't want to go.

"Is he going to bring that woman," Malcolm asked, as he stood brushing his hair in front of his bedroom mirror.

I knew whom he was referring to and knew that the time had come for me to tell them the truth.

"You mean the one who came here?" I asked.

"Yeah," Marcus answered, plopping down on his twin bed.

"Why'd she come here anyway?" Marcus continued.

"Who is she?" Malcolm asked, now throwing a tennis ball against the wall.

I held my hands up, letting them know I needed not to be bombarded.

"She's your dad's girlfriend."

They didn't respond.

"Daddy likes her and . . ."

"Better than you?" Marcus asked.

I looked at Malcolm, who had stopped throwing the ball. He looked away.

"Well, it's different," I said.

"Daddy and I are still friends," I lied. "We'll always be connected through you. We both love you . . ."

Marcus got up from his bed and ran out of the room. Malcolm put down the ball and looked after his brother and then looked at me.

"So what's going to happen now?" Malcolm asked.

I looked at my sweet, soft-faced firstborn, my golden child. I couldn't lie to him, any more than I already had. He knew me too well for that anyway.

"I don't know, baby. I really don't know."

I got up from where I'd been sitting on Malcolm's twin bed.

"I need to go and find your brother."

I found Marcus outside, in the back of the house throwing his beloved basketball at the hoop.

"Aren't you cold? You gonna mess up your clothes."

"I'm not going," he said, pausing to make a free throw.

"Whaddya mean? You love the show and you'll go to your favorite restaurant."

"I don't wanna go and you can't make me."

I inhaled, defeated, knowing the truth of *you can't make me.*

He sank the ball through the net and looked at me. I understood he was mad and wanted to hit something, make somebody, me, feel the pain he was in. Jay was his anchor. Marcus and Jay were the most alike and Marcus had felt especially betrayed by his dad's leaving.

"Oh, baby," I said, reaching out to hug him.

"I'm not a baby," he said, yanking his head and shoulders away from me.

"Don't touch me," he said, throwing the ball down. "I'm not going." He stomped back inside the house.

When Jay arrived Marcus had shed his dress clothes and put on his standard jeans and Camby jersey. He wouldn't look at Jay, who had tried to talk to him. Jay turned to me. I didn't know what to say, other than making a face that said, *what'd you expect?*

"He doesn't want to go with you," I said, after we left Marcus and Malcolm in their room.

"What about Malcolm?"

"Brotherly bond. I don't think he'll go, either."

Jay scratched his head and exhaled defeated.

"So what am I supposed to do with the tickets?"

I looked at him and smirked.

"Shove 'em up your ass."

CHAPTER TWENTY-ONE

The last few months I'd been working for our town's weekly paper, going around town with a question each week, something related to the town, and taking portraits of the respondents. I was nervous at first. I hadn't had a job taking pictures since college, but soon I got the swing of it and didn't want to give it up. Kayreen liked my work enough to offer me a regular part-time job. Meanwhile my life with Jay continued in limbo—no formal separation or divorce papers had been filed, no talk of wanting to marry Julie, just nothing. Jay and I only talked about the children and he came on alternate weekends and took them for the entire time. He had managed not only to give Ivy's party, but he made it spectacular, like being inside pink chiffon. He had balloons and long thin satin ribbons, little Christmas lights, crepe paper streamers all coming from the ceiling fixture and draped over the dining room table. He had a storyteller guitarist. All the neighborhood children were there, he even registered Ivy at a local store. It was a perfect party. I looked at Jay across the dining room, holding Ivy as she pointed to a balloon and him saying the word, *balloon*, teaching her to say it. I felt something inside me loosen.

I came to look forward to the time alone, when Jay had the children. I made Jay promise to not have them around Julie. I couldn't tolerate that, especially given that we were in limbo. My weekends without children allowed me something I hadn't had in over a decade—time to myself. All those little things that I had taken for granted before I became a mother, which had overnight been snatched away from me when Malcolm, Marcus and Ivy were born. Before I became one I'd hear new mothers complain that they didn't even have time to go to the bathroom alone, I couldn't imagine it. I figured they were just poor time managers. That was then, before I'd joined the club, before I was a witness to how much becoming a mother simply changes who you are and you have no time to figure out who you've become, because you have no time. When Jay had the kids, I'd just soak in the tub, stare out the window, read. I found a little line in a book called *The Mask of Motherhood* that Paige had given me that illuminated everything I'd been struggling with: "We've lost the dreadful claustrophobia of living life in a box. But in the process have lost a sense of place. We are a generation in transit: we know exactly where we've been (and good riddance!) but we're not at all certain where we ought to be going."

I used to relegate my mother friends to a separate space in my head and heart, but I realize now that they are more like comrades in arms because motherhood is such a colossal thing to happen to a woman that the shared experience is huge. It was the mental work of it all that was exhausting, the part that fell solely to the woman: arranging all of it. Paige had help, but it was still she (and I and every other mother) who figured out if the baby was teething, had an ear infection, checked developmental milestones and arranged preschools and on and on. I was finally able to hear myself—all the noise and clutter were gone. There's nothing as delicious as a quiet house, especially for a mother of young children. It's more fabulous than sex, lobster drenched in butter served in bed on 560-thread-count sheets.

In addition to the job at the local paper, and the other part-time job, which was at a local gallery and involved giving tours, getting coffee, cataloging and anything that needed to be done. I was, for the first time, putting food on the table. Jay's Harlem business continued to take all his attention, even though he'd claimed it was not profitable and the Pomona office was practically running itself.

I opened the door to get my newspapers off the lawn and was surprised to see Kayreen pulling into my circular driveway.

"You cut your hair!" she said, as she got out of her car. "You look like a coed."

"Well thanks," I said, as we air-kissed at the front door.

"What's up?" I asked her, ushering her inside.

"Jay didn't tell you?"

"Tell me what?"

"That I was coming by?"

"No. I haven't talked to Jay. Coming by for what?"

"For a walk-through . . ."

"A walk-through?"

Kayreen realized that I didn't know about the walk-through and clearly couldn't know that Jay was even thinking about selling.

"Why don't we have a cup of tea," Kayreen said, putting her arm around me, as if she needed to hold me together.

"I need to call Jay," I said, seething.

We went inside, I told her to look around, have a seat, whatever.

I pushed the numbers into the phone and reached him on his cell phone.

"What the fuck do you think you're doing," I said as a way of hello.

"What's the matter, Ina?"

"The matter? What's the fucking matter? Kayreen's here to do a walk-through, dammit, that's what's the matter."

He sighed a loud, disgusted sigh.

"Damn, Ina, I'm sorry. She was supposed to wait until I had a chance to talk to you."

"And what Jay, it just slipped your mind? This is so fucked up . . ."

"I know. I'm really sorry—"

"You're fuckin' right about that, you *are* a sorry muthafucka."

I hit the off button and slammed the phone onto the base.

Kayreen sat me down at my kitchen table. She massaged my neck and shoulders while I sat, furious, unable to speak.

"I know this is hard, baby," Kayreen said, after I'd calmed down enough to sip the chamomile she'd made. "It feels like somebody's just pullin' your guts out. This isn't just a beautiful house, this is your home."

What is it about the word *home* that is so packed, so emotional? I felt my nose burn and hot tears slid down my face, salty as they ran into my mouth. I let them come hard and loud. I cried until my face was dry and my head hurt. I cried as if I were alone.

"I'm sorry to just spring this on you. I never would've come if I'd . . ."

"I know that. You don't have to tell me that."

A separated person in the suburbs is as in demand as a Ford Explorer with Firestone tires. While Paige was always there to help out with the kids, things between us had felt tense ever since the separation, which we'd talked about but not in any depth. It became clear to me why divorced people have to get new friends. Married people are afraid of divorce, like it's a virus they might catch, so they keep their distance. She would ask how I was doing in a way that I knew she knew, and I figured she'd seen the Julie Christmas day show. But I was learning not to care anymore about what people thought. No more Paula Sweet dinner parties, Ashley and Amir cocktails, potluck at book clubbers' homes and I'm sure even the weekly pizza night after soccer practice would soon dry up. The moms continued to invite me but made it clear that I wasn't expected to show up since all the other children were there with both of their parents. They were giving me an out, so I wouldn't feel bad by being there without my spouse. A few years ago when a neighbor had gotten divorced and moved back to the city Paige had flippantly said, "People don't know how to deal with single people in the suburbs." I had no idea how right she was.

Since I'd become a social pariah, I almost looked forward to the baby shower I'd been invited to. I'd forgotten what it was like to get an invitation and could hardly remember what it was like to toss them. So I went, even though in the past staying home cleaning the kitchen sink drain seemed more fun.

I got to the shower and the quartet throwing the shower all seemed so high I began to think, They're all taking black beauties or some other kind of amphetamine. I was starved on my way over, but immediately anger quelled my appetite. Two of the hosts had talked to me about how they can't stand the honoree. I began to feel the funky vibes in the room. I know too much. I knew most of these ostensibly happily married women were living their cushy lives on credit and mirrors; these women who never uttered anything but positives about motherhood—*he's the best thing in my life; I can't imagine my life without children; my life is my children*—had all felt like running away at some point. It was as if they'd watched too much television and were now only capable of mimicking what they'd watched.

Couldn't have real conversations about real feelings because feelings, thoughts, had been purged to make room for their life as a movie. Their ways, their proclamations used to make me feel like a fake. Like I was playing at wife and mommy and they were the real ones, but now I could see them. I could see the way some of them rarely touched or looked at their husbands; how one was oh so polite when she thought someone was listening, but ice cold when she thought they were alone. I finally saw they were all drowning, as I had. How they micromanaged their children's activities instead of having something of their own.

I had tried hard to force myself into this life; the blueprint was to be too busy to think. My mother had always said I was a true Eleazer because I used to think all the time. Entertaining possibilities was just masochistic, at least my baby shower friends believed so—self-examination was simply dangerous and useless. They used to seem utterly blissful by simply zoning out and living life like a movie—design your house, husband and children with a Martha-esque zeal, fill in with activities so the noise of busyness overwhelms anything else. But the show was over, at least for me. I'd seen the man behind the curtain and could no longer will myself to be blind. Don't try to figure out what you're supposed to be doing and do it. Don't fight so hard. There had been a time when that sounded good, but not anymore, not for me.

I stayed long enough to air-kiss the honoree, eat a handful of potato chips with onion dip and give her a present.

TWENTY-TWO

A baby-blue coffin held Zackie's body, which was dressed in a dark blue suit, white shirt, red tie and bad funeral parlor makeup. He would have hated all of it. I wished they had dressed him the way he would have dressed himself, a nice herringbone jacket, a paisley silk ascot, but Aunt Juneann gave in to Uncle Ben, who couldn't, even in death, accept who Zackie was. I sat on the folding chair, pressing my feet onto the grass green indoor/outdoor carpet. A huge heart of red, pink and white gladiolas with a banner that read "Beloved Son," across it sat propped on a stand next to the fern I'd sent. The reality of their denial of him depressed me almost as much as his death. How could he be dead? I just sat there numb, not wanting to even look at him, the smell of the lurid flowers filling my nostrils.

Maybe this was just how it was for people born outside the box. You either had to try to fake it or you died young. Neither option appealed to me.

What was left of my birth family was there: Zackie's parents, Mom, Dad, my cousin Paris, neighbors, Zackie's friends. I felt so alone. It was probably the first time in a very long time that we were all together, with Zackie. I couldn't stay with my grief because my anger at how they didn't let him be who he was in his death kept intruding.

After the service and the family procession out, I saw Jay. He reached out to touch my shoulder and I noticed that his eyes were red.

Outside the funeral parlor—they decided against a church funeral because of his *lifestyle*—Jay came to me and said that he was sorry. We reached out for each other and I let go of my anger, let it all release onto his chest, smelling his familiar fragrance. He handed me a handkerchief, something my daddy used to do, something that I used to make fun of Jay for carrying, so old-fashioned, so middle-class. I was as grateful for that handkerchief as I was to have him there, he was someone who understood how close Zackie and I were, how much pain I was in. My family never approved of my connection to Zackie and secretly felt that I'd somehow influenced his sexuality; that it was my fault that he'd "wanted to be a girl."

It had been nine months since our separation, but seeing Jay among my mismatched ragtag family, Zackie's cross-dressing friends, the ladies dressed in white with paper doilies bobby-pinned to their heads, was like finding my missing piece, my partner, my teammate.

"I miss him so much," I said, as I sobbed into the smooth wool of his suit jacket.

He patted my back, telling me, "I know, I know."

We had a classic *colored* repast at Aunt Juneann and Uncle Ben's that Zackie would've loved. The yams and greens were perfect, the ham and turkey smoked, the beans were various—black-eyed and green and red with rice and even butter. Mom sat with a plate on her lap and seemed relatively lucid for the first time in years, Daddy right next to her encouraging her to eat, making sure she didn't drop any food from her plate. Aunt Juneann was sporting a new short haircut that Uncle Ben wept over when he saw it.

When Zackie died she went to her neighborhood beauty parlor and told her beautician, "Bee, cut it all off." "You sho'?" Bee asked. Aunt Juneann assured her that she was and within minutes the thick braid that hung down her back was in Bee's hand. "You wanna keep it?" At first Juneann said "No thanks," but after she got in the car she thought about it and then went back and got it to give to Ben. Eleazer women knew that men loved hair. "Shit, he can have it, wear it, put it under his damn pillow, shove it up his ass," she thought as she drove away.

Uncle Ben was holding court in the living room filled with people from his job, church and bowling league. After several shots of Jack, he started yelling for Aunt Juneann, who was in the kitchen.

"Baby. Hey, baby! Baby!"

She came into the living room, wiping her hands on her holiday apron.

"What the hell you want, Ben?"

"Where your braid at? I wanna show them all dat hair you cut off, widout even axin' me." He was in big-time slur mode now.

Juneann rolled her eyes, and went back into the kitchen, snatching his glass of Jack Daniel's, taking it with her.

I was not prepared for the thing that happened next: Uncle Ben started crying. First the subject switched from politics—Republicans, Democrats they're the same—just the usual Uncle Ben talking loud, then his eyes got as red as peppers. I figured he was just drunk—which he was—but then he began to talk about Zackie and what a funny kid he was, how smart he'd been, and that's when Uncle Ben started to sob about his boy being gone.

"Zackie coulda been anything. Anything," he cried, voice cracking.

It seemed the more he talked, the more he slurred and the more he cried. Finally Daddy and one of the men from the bowling league gathered up Uncle Ben and took him upstairs to sleep it off.

Family legend has it that when Aunt Juneann—the feistiest of them all—and Ben got together, she seemed like a changed woman. Wasn't so fast to cuss you out. She smiled more. She was always one for dressing up, even when she wasn't going anywhere in particular, and Ben liked his woman to always look good. Aunt Juneann would wear a chiffon polka-dot dress to a baseball game. My mom would tease her, "Where the hell you think you going, over to Mickey Mantle's for a dinner party?" She'd laugh and take a drag on her cigarette, red lipstick bleeding through the tip. Ben was the one she'd always wanted, but she married some- one else first, someone handsome who had a nice car. Prob- lem was, that was all he was. Aunt Juneann and Uncle Ben first met when they were in high school. His folks had just moved to Pomona from North Carolina. He was shy or seemed so. Didn't talk much 'cause the kids would make fun of him and call him country. Juneann thought it made him sound gentle. As rough as she was, she was always drawn to things delicate—orchids, newborns, china. She was just a tender thing underneath, but she, in true Eleazer form, had to create a shell just to survive in our world. Ben was drawn to her, too, but was wary of her at first. She was so pretty and had been popular in high school, always in the middle of everything, he couldn't believe that she'd really be inter- ested in him. But eventually Ben and Juneann became like one word. They married, the Korean War happened and Ben was drafted and when he came back, Juneann waited, as she said she would, but he had started the drinking. Having to wrap his mind around referring to the war as a "conflict," when the things Ben saw: civilians killed, Americans killed by Americans, and scenes that he couldn't shut off . . . He'd fly into violent rages at the littlest thing or sometimes at nothing at all. But she told him she'd never leave him. She was waiting for the old Ben to return.

I went out to the sun porch to take a break from the theater that was my family. The furniture smelled musty, but the air felt good. I looked at the backyard where Zackie and I spent hours as children playing dodge ball and hide-and-seek and lying on our backs looking up at the sky.

"Is this a private party?" Jay said, interrupting my reverie.

He stood in the doorway.

I nodded, but pointed to a spot next to me on the wicker love seat.

"Ina, I'm really sorry about Zackie."

I looked at the doorframe, noticing the peeling paint around the screen door.

"I know how much he meant to you."

"Thanks. I appreciate you coming. You didn't have to."

"I wanted to. I cared about him, too, you know."

I looked at Jay, who had been crying.

"You know, I used to think you were easy to understand, but you're not," I said.

He chuckled.

"Not the simpleton you thought you married, huh?"

I looked at the handkerchief, the one he'd given me that I bunched in my hands.

"You are quite complex, but it's like you don't want to be."

He hunched his shoulders.

"Who knows? Look, I wanted to tell you again that I'm sorry about the house. I should've told you about the business. I should—"

I held up my hand to stop him. To say I didn't want to talk about the house.

"What about the business?" I asked after I realized what he'd said.

"You don't know?"

I looked at him impatiently.

"Know what?"

"I had to close it. I couldn't get a toehold in the Commercial Harlem . . . it never . . ."

"What? I had no idea. How was I supposed to know?"

"I don't know, I figured Kayreen or Paige or somebody would've told you."

"No. I hadn't heard a thing. So that's big."

"Yeah," he said, looking away. "Listen, I need a drink. You want anything?"

I eagerly nodded my head.

He came back with two rock glasses of scotch, something neither of us drank, but this was a scotch-and-beer-drinking crowd. I took a sip of the amber liquid, letting it burn my throat and chest as it went down. I smiled at Jay for having the idea and he smiled back. We were like two kids sneaking alcohol at the grown-ups' party. When something bad happens to someone, the person assumes everyone around them is thinking about it, talking about it, but everyone has their own dramas and are always most concerned with themselves first. So finally Jay laid it out for me himself. He was broke. We were broke. He'd gambled practically everything on the Harlem business and it didn't work. He still had his residential Pomona office, but that was it, and that had been ignored during the last two years as he was focusing on Harlem. Having to sell our house would be only one of the things we'd have to do to survive.

"So are you alright?" I asked.

Jay drained his glass and set it down on a plastic end table.

He rubbed his face and I realized he was holding back tears. Jay cried when we got married, when the children were born, when Malcolm hit his first home run. I'd never seen him cry at anything other than joy.

He inhaled deeply, swallowing his tears.

"I'm not sure, Ina. I'm not sure."

If we had been the old Jay and Ina, I would've put my hand on his, rubbed it and told him everything would be fine. But we weren't the old Jay and Ina and I had no soothing words for him. I'd used them all up on myself.

TWENTY-THREE

K ayreen walked in and immediately began ogling the Biedermeier chest in the front hallway.

"My gosh, this piece is gorgeous."

"Ode to a different time. You wanna buy it?"

"You'd sell it?"

"In a heartbeat."

"I'll think about it. Let's look around."

I took her into the large, sunny living room that took me two years to decorate. The red-rust-striped taffeta curtains puddled at the floor; the yellowish-gold sofa with fringe and deep, comfy down cushions with lots of pillows accented in black and white faced the limestone fireplace; the mantel had topiaries on either side, our wedding picture and silver-framed black-and-white photos of each of the children as infants.

"This room will show very nicely. It's nice and bright, all we'll need to do is add some fresh flowers."

Off the living room was our family room, which hadn't been used much, I realized, since Jay left. The kids had taken to watching TV in their rooms and when I was home I was usually in bed or zonked out on the chaise in my sitting room.

"Rooms smell funny if people don't use them," Kayreen said, when I told her we hadn't been using this one much.

From there I showed her my warm weather oasis—our screened-in porch with the wicker furniture that I'd had dipped in black and for which I'd had custom cushions made from fabric ordered from France.

"More potted begonias for here," Kayreen said, as she wrote in her steno pad.

The dining room was large and very formal with an antique Chippendale table mixed with replica chairs with seating for fourteen.

"What was I thinking," I mumbled.

"This is a fabulous, classic dining room," she said, checking the servants' bell, which had long been disconnected.

"Yeah, other than Thanksgiving, I think we had two sit-down dinner parties the whole time we were here."

Through a swinging door we went into the kitchen—gourmet, Viking, Sub-Zero, Miele, top-of-the-line everything, one year out of my life renovating.

"It's spectacular. This is gonna sell this house. In a weekend."

"No way, you think?"

"Darlin', homes like this are still movin' faster than a

rooster chasing a hen in heat. I guarantee you I'm gonna sell this baby in days."

I felt a little queasy.

"Let's go upstairs. I'm sure the kids' rooms are a mess."

She followed me up the wide staircase, the runner a red leaf pattern that I'd fallen in love with. On the landing beneath the Palladian window sat a teak bench we'd bought on a trip to Singapore. Pillows and plants and children's books sat nearby.

"Ina, you've done a beautiful job with this house."

"Thanks, Kayreen. It was a good distraction."

She looked confused.

I walked through my house, seeing it with her fresh eyes, and I remembered my drive to make it look perfect, convinced that that would make our lives perfect. There'd actually been a time when I thought such was possible. It *was* a beautiful, perfect house—and look at the mess inside the people who lived in it.

Ivy's room was all little-girl pink and white with hints of gold and lace. I'd even done the brown-faced, rosy-cheeked cherub mural myself.

The boys' room was French blue twin beds and green plaid bedding with contrasting blue stripes, which was also the color scheme for the fabric I used to make the curtains. The children's playroom was a large extra bedroom. I'd painted the floors a black-and-white harlequin pattern and lined the walls with paper so they could paint, draw or write whenever they wanted. There were oversize stuffed elephants, a giraffe and a lion and several teddy bears sat in the table and chair set, around which were the boys' train tracks. I used to stand outside this room, just to hear them playing. I rubbed my eyes and Kayreen put her arm around me.

"You okay, sweetheart?"

I'd thought I was fine until she asked and then I started to break down.

"Aw, come here, sugar," she said and enveloped my body in her embrace. "Now, now. Selling your house is a big thing, there there, just let it out."

"I'm sorry," I said, pulling away from her, gathering my composure back. "I don't . . ."

"Listen, you're going through a lot right now. Just give yourself permission."

"Anything you think we have to do to the kids' rooms?"

"Nope, they look beautiful, just a little tidying up. Did you do anything to the third floor?"

"Jay has a—I mean had—an office up there and there's two more bedrooms."

"So there're four down here and three upstairs?"

"Yeah, that's right."

"And you finished the basement?"

"Yeah."

"Beautiful. You're making my job too easy."

"Well, then maybe you can cut your commission."

"Mmm, you *have* learned a thing or two.

"How 'bout I wave the fee on the buy. You are going to buy something else, aren't you?"

"I assume, but it's going to be much smaller."

"Small can be beautiful, honey."

"Small and not grand."

Kayreen looked at me with pity in her eyes.

True to her promise, Kayreen had multiple offers on our house after only a weekend; now we'd have to decide which buyer and find someplace else to live.

Kayreen arrived Monday morning, and I put on a kettle for tea.

"Hon, I wanna show you some specs on houses I've pulled."

I looked around my kitchen and sighed at the thought of all that was facing me.

It's funny how life moves on whether you pay attention or not. We'd lived in this house for so long, I was having a hard time imagining living somewhere else. But change was what we had to do—a new start minus Jay. The kids seemed to be handling things okay. Although Malcolm always seemed fine, Marcus was a little quieter, a little moody, but he was going on ten and in fifth grade, a tough period.

She sat down in the kitchen and looked around.

"This really is a great house, but there's a few interesting things here . . ."

"Interesting. That's a deadly word."

She laughed. "Ina, you are too much."

"Don't ask me to fix anything, paint. The house sells as is . . ."

"Of course, of course."

She asked if I'd heard from Jay.

"Does he want to be in on this or what?"

"He knows we got multiple bids, but I haven't told him anything since," I said.

"Mmm. Have you talked to him?"

"Actually no, we've been playing phone tag."

"*Hmm,*" Kayreen's lips tightened and looked as if she were trying to decide whether to go with the green over the blue tile.

"What's going on?" I asked her.

"Ina, I just don't feel comfortable telling you this."

"Kayreen, spit it out please."

"Well, I heard Jay's business folded last week. The Harlem office, apparently, just wasn't making any money . . ."

"He already told me that."

"He did? Did he tell you about Julie?"

"Julie?" I spat out. "No. We don't talk about her."

She smirked.

"Well, you know I'm not one to gossip . . ."

We both chuckled out loud.

"Well, it seems Miss Jarvis sent Jay packin'."

"You mean they broke up?"

"That's what I heard. I coulda predicted that. I mean, once Harlem went belly up, she wasn't about to hang around for the postmortem."

"So the man loses his business and she dumps him, just like that?"

"That's what I hear," said Kayreen.

"Nice girl."

The whistle blew on the kettle and Kayreen's cell phone rang simultaneously.

"Oh, it's probably the rich clients from hell."

TWENTY-FOUR

"Does this mean we're poor?" Marcus asks from the backseat.

I'd driven the children by the house we were buying, a small, butterscotch-colored stucco craftsman with overgrown vinca flowing from the window boxes. The dark green shutters had been straightened, but slats were missing. It needed work.

"Does it have a basketball hoop," Malcolm wants to know.

"It doesn't, but we can put one up," I say, sounding like Marsha Brady.

I look through the rearview mirror at Ivy sleeping in her car seat, her mouth agape, clutching her favorite Beanie Baby frog.

"There's a screened-in porch and a patio and a nice yard, just like our old house."

"Can we see it?" the boys say in unison.

"When we officially buy it, then you can look all around, okay?"

They're placated. I think.

"You didn't answer my question," Marcus says, irritated this time.

"What question is that?" I ask, knowing full well what he's talking about.

"Are we poor now?"

"What does that mean to you? Poor?"

"No money," Malcolm says before rapping: "Broke, like poke, eatin' poke and beans, keepin' leans, what it means."

I sigh.

"Well, I don't think we'll be eating pork and beans, at least not every night, but we don't have a lot like we used to."

"Is that 'cause Daddy left?" Marcus asks, his tone slightly less angry.

"No, it's not 'cause Daddy left. It's the way the world is now and Daddy had to close one of his offices and I don't make a lot of money at my jobs . . ."

"So we *are* poor," Marcus says.

"Maybe I should get a job," Malcolm adds.

I'm so grateful for this kid. I look at him through the rearview and smile. His face earnest, he beams back at me.

"You can get a paper route if you want. This is a small house and it has everything that we need. We can make it pretty."

*　　*　　*

I got to the diner first and took a seat at a familiar booth. Jay had suggested that we meet outside to talk—especially since our house was filled with half-packed boxes.

The same waitress that we'd had as a family a hundred times gave me a menu and acknowledged me like I might've been there before. I refused to let that bother me. It was my new turning-forty stance in the world—refusing to let anything other than the three most important things in my life get to me.

Jay walked in dressed in a seersucker jacket and creamy linen pants. He hadn't been sleeping but still looked like every other prosperous black guy who'd gotten rich and smoothed his patina down to nothing. He had that perfection thing going—the haircut and groomed like a model in an *Ebony* ad for Murray's pomade, the skin sanitized of any blackheads, razor bumps sanded down. The crease of his trousers like a blade, draping just so, and while he looked fine enough to sip, this look was not something that turned me on. I like frayed edges, discolored fabric worn from experience. I like a patina. "Perfection is the voice of the oppressor." I forgot where I read it, but I'd written it in my journal. Jay had become even shinier since hanging out with Julie, I guess. I sorta liked when he was a bumpkin-ish guy who occasionally mispronounced words.

"I like the haircut," he said, as he slid into the booth. "You look like a Howard girl I used to know."

I couldn't help but smile. He always knew what to say to break anyone down.

"Did you order?" he said.

"Nope, I was waiting for you."

The waitress came over, greeted Jay like an old friend and took our orders.

"So do you wanna look at this house today? I can call Kayreen."

"Sure, sure," he said.

I realized since he wouldn't be living there he probably didn't care that much what the house looked like, but since he was paying for most of it, it seemed like a good idea.

"Where is it?"

"On Waterbury."

"Oh, that's a nice street. Good bones?"

I chuckle.

"It's the worst house on the block," I said.

"I'm sure it's fine. Listen, Ina, I'm sorry about all this mess."

I couldn't be sure what exactly he was apologizing for. There had been much, and right now I didn't really care about how bad he felt. I didn't feel angry, didn't feel anything, just wanted to move on to what was next.

"How're the kids doing with it?"

"They wanna know if we're poor now."

"What'd you say?"

"Broke, not poor."

"Oh, that's good. I like that. 'Broke not poor.' How are you handling leaving? I know how much you loved that house."

"You did, too."

"Yeah," he said, almost in a whisper, to himself.

The funny thing was, it wasn't as difficult as I would've imagined. In some ways I was looking forward to living in a "normal" house. Ours always took too much to maintain, to fill up and warranted too much comment, which used to feel like pressure, either the size, the color, the neighborhood, distance from the street. Or worse was when old friends would come over and say nothing—not, "This is a big house, a nice house or a bright house," but nothing at all. The nothings were worse because you just knew they were thinking something and the fact that they'd made the decision to keep whatever they were thinking to themselves said more about them than I wanted to know.

"So have you seen a lawyer yet?" I said bluntly.

Our soups came and Jay put his napkin in his lap and picked up his spoon.

"Well, no. I'm not really thinking about that."

"Well, we need to be thinking about something. Limbo's not a place I want to stay in."

I ate a spoonful from my soup, not sure why I said that. I hadn't much thought about this limbo state or about divorce, either. I guess I was just trying to force him to do something.

"Can we take care of one thing at a time?" he said, trying not to sound impatient.

As I sat looking at Jay in his entire nouveau splendor, I couldn't help thinking about the fundamental problem between us: he aspired to being in the box and I'd discovered that I couldn't breathe in it. I'd been born into what Jay aspired to and Julie Jarvis even more so. Were we both just affects, like the Biedermeier chest in the front hall? Put there because it made just the right statement for people entering the house? This is who we are; we have this huge, beautiful home with exquisite taste. As successful as he was he still saw himself as a boy from the Hollow who was never welcomed at those Ashley and Amir ski trips or pool parties. As soon as our kids began losing their baby teeth he started pressing me about putting them in Ashley and Amir. I didn't want to see that in him, that person with his face pressed against the glass, wanting to belong to something, some group that didn't want him, that didn't know him. He was fine without all that, even better because everything he'd gotten he'd earned. He had no connected parents who could make a call for him or college-educated ones who already had a foot on the rung of social mobility. He'd had to do it all himself and that made him extraordinary. Maybe now that he'd lost almost everything, he would learn that.

"So what're your plans now?" I asked.

He sipped his Coke and quietly burped into his napkin.

"You mean about the business?"

I nodded.

"I'm going to run this one, move back here. Start again, which is what I really wanted to talk to you about."

"I'm all ears."

"I hope it won't be too weird having me living in Pomona again."

I was silent for a while, enough to make him squirm.

"Oh, I get it, she drops you and you run back home?"

He looked surprised.

"What're you talking about?"

"I heard Julie kicked you to the curb."

"You did? Well, whoever your supplier is, you better tell them to do better research."

"What do you mean?"

"Just what I said. Julie and I broke up, but she didn't do the breaking."

I finished my lunch and ordered a cup of coffee. I wanted to be fully alert for this tale.

Jay told me that Julie was pressing him to begin divorce proceedings. She wanted to be engaged by next summer so her family could throw a big party on the beach in Sag Harbor.

"I started thinking about our little wedding and about those early years in Brooklyn and how we used to be happy . . ."

We *used* to be happy.

". . . And I realized I didn't want to be thinking about starting again . . ."

"Yeah, you figured, better not jump out of the pan and into the fire . . ."

I knew I was being bitchy, but I couldn't help it. It felt so good.

"No, that's not what I was thinking," he said angrily. "Look, let's deal with the house business. Call Kayreen and have her meet us there."

CHAPTER TWENTY-FIVE

P aige showed up the day before the move with dinner.

"I figured you didn't have a chance to think about food," she said, walking past me with dinner in one shopping bag and rolls of bubble wrap and newspaper in another.

"You're a lifesaver."

"It's just some chicken and potatoes and salad, but . . ."

"It's great, thanks. Come on in, watch yourself."

We settled on the living room sofa.

"So Waterbury, huh? It's not that far," she said.

"No. An ambitious walk."

"Gosh, it's gonna be weird not having you next door. The kids are already melting down."

"Mine, too, but I know they'll still get together."

"Yeah, but it'll be different, though . . . when you can't just run next door."

"Yeah. You've been a great neighbor, Paige. I couldn't have gotten through this without you."

"Aw, stop. I didn't do anything special. Listen, I just want you to know I'm still here. Anything you need—contacts, a plumber, somebody to fix your car—you just call me, you hear? I mean it."

"I know, I know. I will. Will you stay and have some of this with me? The kids are with Jay."

"I'll stay while you eat. I'll have some salad."

I unwrapped the platter of food.

"So how's the photography going?"

"Good. I set up my website and I'm actually getting bites, still haven't been commissioned on my own yet . . ."

"You will. You know, Ina, I admire you."

"Paige, please. Me?" I said, cutting a breast of rosemary chicken before stabbing the baby potatoes with leaks. "Mmm, this is delicious. I wish I could cook like this."

Paige blushed and waved away my compliment. "I've got the time."

"Yeah, well, I definitely don't have much of that anymore," I said, biting into a lemon and poppy-seed muffin.

"I really do admire what you've done. You just got yourself together when Jay . . ."

"Left? Come on, you can say it."

Sometimes married people treat separation and divorce like a contagious illness.

"Yeah. I mean, I've seen this happen to many a woman and it crushed them."

"Well, thanks for saying that. Of course, I don't see my-self that way."

"Well, you should. You should feel pretty proud of your-self."

Being crushed was not an option for me, I thought, but didn't say. It was the thing that was different between black and white women: she always had someone and something to fall back on, a husband and if not him, a fa-ther, a brother and so on. It was part of the background, the entitlement of a white woman in a culture where that means something. I am a black American woman and we don't come with those kinds of backgrounds. Our histori-cal landscape never granted us such, my sisters had to rely on themselves because their man could be beaten and killed on any given day, taken away without word or warning. Working? We always worked and took care of business in the fields, and of our kids and other people's, too. I flashed on Aunt Juneann raising cousin Paris when her own mother couldn't. I flashed on my grandmother picking up and leaving the South with a baby growing in-side her and one on each hand. Alone, scared, but not crushed and not about to be. That kind of will was borne in my bones, just as my big thighs, thick hair and bad teeth were.

We stayed on safe topics. Even though I knew Paige, herself, was a working-class girl from Indiana and didn't come from privilege, there was still an inheritance granted for simply being white. I understood that and so did she, even though she'd rarely admit it—preferring to or need-ing to focus on the fact that there were plenty of whites that hadn't come from means, who had had to struggle, who still do. We had, over the years, agreed to see things from our own perspective but to respect the other's position. It was the only way we were to move from neighbors to friends.

Years earlier, when Paige's mother was dying, I learned later from liver disease caused by her sometimes skid-row-level alcoholism, I looked after her children for three weeks even though at the time she had a competent housekeeper. I went over their homework, made sure their meals were nutritious and even took them to their various sport activities and cheered them on if their dad couldn't. She never forgot it. When she came back, raw from having spent so much time with the ghosts she thought she'd left back home, she shared her story of being on scholarship when she met her trust-fund husband at college and how it was love almost at first sight, though their getting together was hardly storybook.

Tonight we talked about the people who had bought our house, some bond trader and his wife who were expecting their first child.

"It's an awfully big house for two people and a baby," I said, looking around, remembering how huge it seemed to us when we bought it.

"Guess they're planning to fill it up. What's she like?" Paige asked, eagerly.

"Young."

"Oh gosh. How young?"

"Young. Like maybe thirty."

"Oh my gosh. A baby. What about him?"

"Wall Street. A big swinging one."

"Great. He and Andy will hit it off."

"Oh, Andy's a sweetie."

"Most days."

I knew she was dying to know but would never ask about Jay and our status. Paige wouldn't ask anything she thought might seem like prying or would yield information that would make anyone uncomfortable.

We hardly ever had frank discussions about race after the car theft and now that we were moving, I was sure that we wouldn't. We'd exchange Christmas cards; see each other for coffee occasionally, probably less the longer we're no longer neighbors. She'll find a way, a bridge, to the new, albeit young and dumb, people.

Moving day fell on an unusually cool, late August day. I was grateful for that, since we were doing a lot of the moving ourselves, with a few friends helping. I'd begun to do all of my own lifting—carrying my own water. I've learned that there are two kinds of contemporary women: those who carry their own water and those who don't—they have parents, husbands, brothers, sisters who do all the work for them.

At the end of the day my body ached. The move took all day and everything that I had. The boys fell asleep on a mattress on their bedroom floor. Ivy slept in my room, upstairs in her playpen, as I sat on the floor in my new living room, sipping a very nice zinfandel and feeling my weary bones. I was too tired to sleep. Two interns from my gallery job had just left after bringing wine and helping me unpack a few pieces and put some dishes away. They did enough to keep me from hyperventilating at the thought of too much to do. As I sat on the floor, sipping the wine from a mug, my eyes landed on an unfamiliar box with *attic* scrawled across the side. I punctured the tape with a steak knife and found some large manila envelopes, *Hilltop* stuff on top of some cheap stuffed animals, several college yearbooks and two used textbooks. I opened one envelope and found a small stack of eight-by-ten black-and-whites of a Step Show that'd I'd shot for the paper, my first homecoming. There were the Kappas with their candy-striped canes, the Alphas pressed in their Joe College sweaters and the Ques with their dog chains around their necks. There was Jay. Mid jump, hands in fists, having just pounded his chest; his face was gleaming. He was euphoric—full of life. I let my finger trace his brow where sweat beaded, his hair cut to his scalp. Was this the best time of our lives? I'd offered this picture to Jay a hundred years ago and then I forgot about it. He'd love to have it. He was so happy then, I guess we all were. I looked at this face, these faces, and thought about what happens to people. Do we really change or does life, circumstance force us to adjust ourselves to fit in, just to get up in the morning? My mother, Zackie, Jay, me, all of us wearing some form of shell. Wearing it so long that it just becomes a part of you; it becomes you and the real you evaporates like mist. Or does it? The Jay I remember from campus always smiled and said hello, how's it going, you have a good day. He was always pleasant, positive. He made people see the best part of themselves. He never cared, as David did, about being seen as too nice or soft or unsophisticated because he spoke to people he didn't know—he didn't feel one had to be a social equal to acknowledge another human being. He didn't believe in social equals. He'd been like that when we first married—before he decided to become a mogul. What a strange word that is, it makes you think only of other strange words—ghoul, mongrel. I found other pictures: my first show at the school—fourteen pictures preciously entitled "In the Mood," of people around campus lost in thought or each other. Not too bad, I thought, for a novice. The blacks were dark, the grain was good, shadows, not too bad. There was a senior dance, a homecoming queen coronation, freshmen moving into the Quad—parents' cars lined up, double-parked on Bryant Street, outside the Quad. Not bad. There were dozens of pictures like this. There are pictures of David— never smiling; shots of Leelah, camping it up usually; one caught her off guard, studying on the second floor of the Blackburn Center, perfect for the morning light coming through the floor-to-ceiling windows, dust motes in a sunbeam halo around her Afro puff.

There had been a time when I owned my life and now I felt like I was coming around to myself again. It's like I finally discovered bones in myself I never knew I had. I've discovered that it takes bravery to be one's self. I now know that the only thing I needed to be afraid of was of not finding my true self and having the courage to be me.

In some ways black people are lucky not to be able to pass, to have to be somewhat self-defining, because accepting what the culture hands us is unacceptable. But some people can change the markers, change things around—names, backgrounds and faces—and fit into ruling society. Change the marker and change your life. Simple as that, well, till you have to look in the mirror. Till forty-something rolls around and that person you've become either gets offed by the real one who's been tied up inside all these years or your sleep becomes permanent, like a death except you just keep breathing. The person I've been pushing down has decided, *you ain't gone have no more peace, okay.* The fuckin' jig is up, baby, and *I'm coming out* . . . and like Miss Ross, *I want the world to know.*

I was turning forty and didn't really want the world to know that, not that I felt badly about it. I didn't, but I didn't want a party. I was excited by the idea of finally, really being a grown-up. Nothing about forty says "still a kid"—unless the person speaking is seventy. What did it mean? That I was no longer juicy; my boobs didn't bounce, I had postbaby, middle-age belly that no amount of sit-ups would flatten and I could stand to loose fifteen, twenty pounds, but I had good, acne-free skin and inside, inside was where the important stuff was. I was less full of shit and less able to tolerate it from other people. I could see through others now, I could see what was real and what wasn't; what was for me and what I needed to run from, no matter how many others were running toward it. Finally, all the things I'd tried in my thirties when I was depressed and delusional about my life I've let go of. It was great to not need to spend $500 for a blouse in order to feel like somebody.

*   *   *

A woman named Marina Henkle runs the gallery where I work. After years of running other people's SoHo galleries along with her husband, mothering four children while living in the 'burbs, she decided to open her own right in Pomona. Before Jay and I separated, almost a year now, I had wandered in there one day with Ivy in the stroller, killing time until Marcus finished his karate lesson. Marina and I got to talking. She liked something I'd said to Ivy—don't recall what—and we hit it off. I told her I used to be a photographer, had worked briefly at the Corcoran, and she offered me a job, just like that. Never saw a résumé or asked for a reference. I liked that about Marina, she lived by her hunches. She ended up with more information about me anyway, by not asking, which is usually the way it is, but most people are too impatient to place you in a context, to get the details of someone's life instead of letting things just appear. Marina's mantra about life was: "It's all about passion, being passionate about your work." Whether it's being a corporate CEO or working at a Laundromat, you've gotta be into what you're doing, otherwise life is going to just grind you down.

She'd forced me to think about all that business of changing my major when I was in college; clearly, I'd stumbled upon what I was really passionate about. What I didn't know then was that photography was all I ever wanted to do, but also that becoming a photographer scared me more than anything because of the possibility that I wasn't good enough. I didn't know then, in college, that I would have to fight for the right to live my passion and that being good at it wasn't even the point. I should've stood up to Leaver, told her college wasn't about getting training to get a job, about safety, should have told her that I, while her daughter, was not her.

"If you don't have passion in your work, you'll become a drama junkie, creating dramas of nothing. It's why people gossip, shop, have love affairs, no passion in their lives, no work," Marina had said that day we met.

After I began working for her, I finally got the nerve to show her some of my work. She offered to show one of my pieces in an upcoming show.

CHAPTER TWENTY-SIX

Jay and Kayreen showed up at my new front door at the same time.

"New homeowner bubbly," she said, holding out a pretty bottle of Perrier-Jouet.

"Um, thanks," I said, letting the two of them in.

"I got a little something for the kids, too, but they're not wrapped. You can just tell them they're from me," she said, handing me a bright orange-and-purple shopping bag.

She'd bought a basketball hoop for the boys and a Groovy Girl for Ivy.

"Kayreen, that was very thoughtful of you," Jay said. "The boys wanted a basketball hoop."

"I figured."

Jay had brought muffins and coffee and pushed aside

some crumpled newspaper to put them on a kitchen counter.

"Kayreen, you can have my coffee. I've already had two cups," Jay said.

"No, honey. I'm runnin', I just wanted to drop off these goodies." She walked over to Jay and patted him on the shoulder. "Ina, can you walk me out to the car, hon?"

"Sure," I said, lifting the plastic lid from the coffee to take a sip. "Jay, I'll be right back."

"Go on . . . kids upstairs?"

"Yeah, they're supposed to be putting away their things."

I followed Kayreen to the driveway on the side of our new house, which we shared, with our neighbor.

"So Jay's bringing breakfast?"

"You didn't get me out here for that."

"Well, you two seem friendly. How's it going? Is he going to move back in? Are you talking about it?"

"We're friendly and that's all," I said.

"Well, I guess now that Julie's flown the coop . . ."

"Or Jay."

"Whaaat? What'd you hear?"

"Kayreen, dear, I really should get back to my cleaning. I've got so much to do. Thanks for the gifts."

I walked away and left her standing in the driveway, dying to know more. I wasn't sure why I'd felt the almost primal need to defend Jay.

"I'll call you later," she yelled as I closed the door.

Jay was already outside setting up the ladder to put up the basketball hoop. Malcolm held the ladder while Marcus dribbled and Ivy clapped and yelped in her stroller. I tried to remember the last time I'd seen Jay do something manual around the house. Looking at them, through the window, I saw a family.

After he was finished and started the boys on a game of one-on-one, he came inside to cold coffee.

"Sorry, microwave's missing."

"That's all right. I'll have a muffin," he said, sitting on a box across the kitchen table from me. "So how do you like the house?" he asked, looking around the sad little kitchen.

"It's not so bad. Nothing some paint and tile won't fix. We'll have to get used to being closer together."

"Yeah, Malcolm and Marcus were complaining about sharing a room . . ."

"They shared a room before . . ."

"I pointed that out. They said that was because they wanted to and now they have to."

"Oh, what brats. This is the way most people live; actually, most people would think this is quite nice," I said.

He smiled a weak smile.

"Guess I gotta get used to being poor, I mean, broke, too."

This didn't sound like the Jay I knew, but he was clearly feeling defeated.

"Thanks for putting up that basketball net."

I wasn't interested in propping him up.

"Oh sure, no problem." Jay took a bite from his muffin. "Do you remember when we were in therapy?"

"Duh? Where'd that come from?"

"I don't know. I was just thinking . . . do you remember what you said, about what that, that guy did to you?"

"Of course."

"We never talked about that."

"What was there to say?"

"I guess I've wondered if you would've married me if it hadn't happened."

"Why are we talking about this now, Jay?"

He turned away from the table and began unwrapping bubble wrap from a plate.

"I don't know. It was just something I was thinking about on my way over."

"I've thought about it, what happened that night, I mean. I've thought about it in terms of where I ended up, living like this instead of in the East Village somewhere . . ."

"Do you regret it?"

"I regret a lot of things, being too trusting for one, but not having a family."

I looked in the direction of the driveway, where the ball was hitting the pavement.

"How could I ever regret that?"

I'd had all three of my children by cesarean section. They were each close to nine pounds and I have a pelvis that doesn't widen very much. Fifty years ago, I would've died in childbirth. Each time I'd tried to have them vaginally, each time I'd endured labor without medication for the pain, believing all the literature about drugs during labor leading to C-sections. It was the first time in my life that my will couldn't overwhelm something—I'd done much by my will, again, an Eleazer trait. Willfulness—it can be a good thing or it can make your life hell. Marcus is willful and has now decided he's not doing his homework.

"Homework's for the dumb kids. I know the stuff, I don't need to do homework," he says to me. Jay talks to him, yells at him, cajoles him, threatens to beat him (in fact he has several times), but Marcus won't cry or give in. Willfulness was what got me through this last year without Jay. But willfulness was what also put me into my sleep for the last ten years—willingness to not deal with my own life, not carry my own water, willingness to just let Jay do our life. Now I won't let him do anything. He offered to deal with the oil company to set up deliveries, I refused; same with getting a painter, plumber, roofer—I did all of it, dealt with all of them, haggled until I got what I thought a fair price. Our new neighbor needed to be spoken to about her pit-bull. I wouldn't let Jay do that either. And it felt good.

Ever since I'd become a mother of school-age children, the beginning of September always felt more like the beginning of a new year. I was looking forward to all the newness—Malcolm was starting high school, Marcus middle school and Ivy was going to day care. With two part-time jobs equaling one full-time job, I was in that hard-to-reach state of being busy, but not totally overwhelmed. I'd begun to meditate and things were just calmer and clearer and even when they weren't it didn't bother me like it used to. I was learning to live and even enjoy uncertainty. I was trying to like having to rein in the spending and living in a much less lavish environment. The old place—while I loved it—caused too much anxiety. I worried about the kids breaking stuff or getting paint on our English custom kitchen cabinets or antiques. I sold most of our old furniture and got rid of worry. Now they paint, lounge, play all over the house and I love not caring if something gets broken. Unfortunately, the same couldn't be said for Jay. He needed to see himself as affluent, moneyed. He loved all the first-class privileges his money had earned—deference from shopkeepers in town, people being impressed when they drove up to our house, belonging to the swim club. All of it soothed the rejected little boy from the Hollow.

Jay finished unwrapping plates and asked rhetorically what else I wanted him to do.

"How about I clean the kitchen and look for the microwave."

"Be my guest, you know the kitchen has become my least favorite place in the house," I happily confided.

Jay began moving about the kitchen, running water, adding detergent, wiping counters and cleaning drawers.

"Looks like they had it cleaned before they left. That's always decent."

"Yeah, remember when we bought the old house, how filthy it was?"

"Boy, that was a lesson. They had money and no class."

I always knew those things didn't automatically go together, but it was something Jay was just learning. Better late than never, I thought. I was also glad to see that he'd rediscovered his domestic ability.

"I'm going up to work on the bedrooms." I got up to leave.

"Ina?"

I turned to look at him.

He seemed to reconsider what he was going to say.

"Let me know if you need some help upstairs."

I walked to him and kissed him on the cheek.

"Thanks, Jay."

Our separation was a funny thing. After the initial shock and anger, I was now discovering that I liked not having to talk over every single thing I did, every decision, whether they did their homework, what the karate instructor said, what Ivy's pediatric visit was like, were they getting enough green vegetables, did they need a bath. The boys were old enough to do all their own body maintenance. They could prepare frozen foods and clean up after themselves. I was merely their driver now, sometimes their priest, still personal assistant. Ivy was on a schedule, she blissfully slept through the night and once she was down the rest of the evening was mine. I liked not having the quiet filled up with the drone of the TV or answering the phone just because it rang. Now when the children were in bed I often sat in silence, reading or just staring at a lit candle. I'd learned to put all that busyness away and just be still.

I invited everyone I knew to the show at Marina's gallery. Leelah came up from D.C. and gave me an orchid. Jay was there with the kids, my mom—lucid—and dad, Kayreen, Paula Sweet and some of the dinner party crew, including my affair minus his wife, Paige and her husband, Andy, even David showed up.

Marina's gallery was wedged between a store that sold expensive antique reproductions and a popular used bookstore. The building had been a garage and maintained one original brick wall where we hung most of the metal and ceramic art. The show was called What I See and featured art photographs by local photographers. My photograph was one of a squirrel on its hind legs, paws perched, as if it were begging for food like a dog. I was nervous and thrilled. It was the time of year when fall has clearly settled in but some days could be eighty degrees. I wore a jersey dress to my ankles, suede boots and a necklace on loan from Marina that looked like a museum piece—five strands of various silver, gray and black pearls. I was hot, but instead of looking sweaty I glowed. I didn't know what to make of all the attention, didn't know if I liked it or not. What was great was the look on Malcolm and Marcus's faces. They were proud of me and that was priceless. Proud of me was sort of the theme of the night. Jay had whispered it in my ear, as had Leelah and Mama.

"You really do have an eye," Mom said.

I thought I was going to cry.

The crowd buzzed and drank champagne served on trays bused by Pomona High School students, some with magenta hair, all with some kind of tattoo and facial piercing.

David walked over to me immediately after another photographer in the show walked away.

"So you're back in your comfort zone, huh?"

Again I'd handled things poorly with him after I'd left

D.C. We'd had several terse phone conversations since I'd been back home, resulting with him demanding I make some kind of future plan with him and me simply refusing. After I'd fantasized over the years about being with him, now that he was offering himself, I had to deal with what I knew about David, the reason it wouldn't have worked years ago. The reality that I'd finally come to understand about David was that he could never have loved the me that I've become. He loved the unformed, fawning girl I had been and some part of me knew I would one day own myself, become the who I am now. I didn't know that then, in D.C. when I left the first time after graduation. And I didn't know it a year ago. But there was something inside me, whispering that, while I loved him, he wasn't the one. And now I know. I wanted to believe him when he said I was the only one he'd ever loved, ever really wanted, but another part of me wouldn't let me buy it. Too much time had passed since our time in college. I would always love some part of him, a part of us from those lovely, uncomplicated days, but it had been over between us for many years. I'd made a life and lives with someone else.

"I don't think it's me you want," I'd said. "I think you just need to win. To be able to say that I chose your way."

"How could you say that? You know that I love you. Don't you know that?"

"I think you think you do." It had been the last conversation we'd had.

"I'm hardly in a comfort zone. I'm surprised to see you here," I said, sipping champagne, feeling happy bubbles running through me.

"Well, I had to be in New York. I got the postcard and figured what the hell."

Well-wishers—PTA members, a few of the kids' teachers—came up, touched me on the arm, offering congratulations.

"Oh yeah, for what?" I said, turning my attention back to him.

"Job interview. ABC thinks my face should be seen."

"You're kidding. Are you going to take it?"

"I'm thinking about it. The *Post* got sold. I think it could be a good time to leave D.C. You wanna come meet me for breakfast?"

"When?"

"Early tomorrow."

"David, I can't."

"You can't, Ina, or you won't?"

I decided to ignore him.

"Well, how about a drink tonight, afterward?"

I looked around the room, not wanting to have this conversation now, but knowing it had to be done.

"I don't want to."

He looked as if I'd hit him in the windpipe.

David was now several years past forty. His life was neat and efficient and he was still not having a committed adult relationship. He didn't know what it was like to have other considerations—would he have been able to learn?

"Well, that was clear."

David recouped his cool.

Leelah came over, breaking into what was becoming an increasingly uncomfortable situation.

"So David, surprised to see you here. Having fun?" she said, grabbing a crab ball from a passing tray.

Not waiting for his answer she turned to me and asked if I needed anything.

"What a fun party and the kids are so cute. That Ivy is too much . . . where'd you find that outfit?" Leelah babbled on.

"Jay bought it for her, for tonight."

"So Jay's the man again, huh," David practically sneered.

"Well, I don't know about that, but he does have good taste," Leelah said.

"I heard the Harlem thing didn't quite work out," he said.

"No, it didn't. . . ." I said.

"So David, when you heading back to D.C.?" Leelah interrupted me.

"Tomorrow, an early shuttle," he snapped.

"Newspaper salaries have gotten better? I'll be on Amtrak."

David didn't respond, but looked as if he smelled spoiled fish.

"Did you see Ina's piece. Isn't it great?" Leelah said.

David, realizing he was acting like a cretin, said: "Oh yes, I was just telling her how good it is that she's finally getting back to her first love."

"Really? Is that what you were saying?" she asked.

I didn't like the feeling of standing next to him. He wasn't used to not getting his way, and I wanted to get far away from the poison he was emitting. I grabbed another flute of champagne and left the two of them to spar.

Jay stood in the center of the room, Ivy on his shoulders looking like the baby of the world. The boys were huddled at the food table, tasting canapés and making faces before stuffing the discards into cocktail napkins. People had begun to leave and, David's behavior notwithstanding, I didn't want the night to end.

Marina came over, her bright red hair cut in a perfect bowl, beaming.

"You've sold your first piece."

I hadn't even entertained the idea of selling my work. I was just thrilled to show it.

"Really? Someone is going to pay actual currency, or do I pay them?" I said.

"No, someone actually paid a few dollars for it and he wants to meet you. Come," she tilted her head as if coaxing a reluctant child.

I followed Marina to a man with a trench coat thrown over his shoulders. He was the principal at the middle school.

"Mrs. Robinson, your work is lovely," he said, extending his hand.

"Oh, Ina, please call me Ina."

"Ina, your work is . . ."

"Thank you, you're so sweet to say so and to come," I said, taking my hand back.

"You know, my wife is on the board at the museum. We've been collectors for some time. Nothing big, but it's what we enjoy."

"Well, I'm flattered to be part of your collection."

"Do you have more work we could see?"

"Of course she does," Marina interrupted. "I'd be happy to set up a showing for you and your wife."

Marina, ever smooth, handed him her card and told him she would call early next week to set up a time.

I thanked him again and went to find my group.

CHAPTER TWENTY-SEVEN

Jay had made reservations at my favorite cheap Thai place after the show for the children, Leelah and I.

"So what was David doing there?" Leelah said to me as soon as we were seated.

"I don't know. I sent him a postcard, but I didn't think he was going to come."

"So why send him an invite?"

"I guess I just wanted him to see what I was doing, that I was doing something with my life, something that he could relate to . . ."

"*Mmm-hmm.*"

"What?"

"Oh nothing. I just don't understand what the unfinished business is with David, that's all."

Jay came back from the bathroom with the boys.

"What're you all talking about?" he said, handing Ivy her Beanie Baby frog as she sat in a high chair.

"Oh, the show. What're we going to eat? The food looks great," Leelah said. "I like your little town. It's much funkier than I expected."

"Thanks, Leelah, although I'm not sure that's a compliment," Jay said.

"Jay's not into funky," I said.

"That's not true," he protested good-naturedly.

After dinner Jay went home to his rented apartment, within walking distance to his real estate office. Leelah came back to the house with the children and me. I had been looking forward to having her spend the night, having something of a pajama party, except now I was too tired from too much standing, talking and too much champagne. After putting Ivy in her crib without a bath and not feeling guilty, I went downstairs to where Leelah was to sleep on the pullout. We went from having two guest rooms to none.

"You need anything, another blanket?"

"No, this is good, this room is so cozy. I like the house."

"Yes, it's coming along. It's very different from the old place," I said, looking at the freshly painted sage walls.

"I'm sure, *le mansion.*"

"I'm so glad you came tonight. It meant a lot to me," I said, hugging her as we sat on the sofa bed.

"I wouldn't have missed your reentry into the art world."

"Well, I wouldn't call it all that," I said. "So how're things with Serena?"

Leelah hunched her shoulders and said fine.

"You know, we're an old married couple now."

"Don't tell me you're feeling that?"

"Yeah, I am. Why, lesbians are immune from marital static?"

"No, I . . ."

"I know, but no one's immune. If you're with one person no matter who she is or you are, you'll get bored sometimes," Leelah said.

It was a revelation. I'd always thought you only got bored if you were with the wrong person.

She lightly slapped my leg.

"Help me make up the bed."

Leelah has always been so sure, so bright, so *so*. If she was feeling bored in her relationship, everyone must, because if there were a way not to that existed in the universe Leelah would've discovered it. Having her back in my life was like getting one of those warm sunny days in December. An ethereal gift I wanted to hold in my hand.

We stood at opposite ends of the foldout and tucked the yellow sheet and then covered it with a white top sheet, a cotton blanket and a down comforter that I'd had for a decade.

"You seem really good," Leelah said, as I smoothed the covers.

I looked at her and smiled.

"I feel good, better than I have for a long time."

"So what're you going to do about David?"

"What do you mean?"

"I mean are you going to finally put that to rest?" she asked.

I looked past her, to the window outside where a raccoon circled my neighbor's garbage can.

"I think we were just not meant to be."

"And you feel bad about that?"

"In a way. I mean, look at him, he's beautiful and smart and sexy and compassionate and everything, but . . ."

"You couldn't let yourself live the fantasy."

"Is that ever possible?"

"You know my opinion. He's also spoiled, selfish, egomaniacal."

I half nodded, more acknowledging what she was saying than agreeing, although I did.

"And what about brother Jay?"

I sat down on the bed. Leelah was seated cross-legged on the floor, running her hand across the rayon pile that looked like sisal.

"What about him?"

"He's trying really hard. Maybe getting kicked in the ass has been good for him," she said.

"*Humph*, I haven't really thought about it. I don't know that there's anything I need to do about him."

"You don't?"

She said it in that accusatory way people have when they know you're not telling the truth. I wasn't up for a debate or even a long discussion, as happy as I was to have her here. I was past that age when we could stay up half the night talking.

"I'm beat, darlin'."

"Me, too, but you know that I know you're full of shit."

I got my tired body up off the sleeper sofa and pecked her cheek good night.

"See you in the morning."

I parked my Outback between two green mini-vans and noticed a perfect yellow Lab sitting obediently on the lawn across the street, while painters scraped the old Victorian. My neighbor waved as she was scurrying off to work, flat backpack on, commuter mug in hand. I'd dropped Ivy at day care and come home to dress before heading to work. Jay took the boys to school. Often, they went to his office after school, did their homework and he brought them home in time for dinner.

We had a routine. We split the mortgage and I scraped together enough to pay for pretty much everything else. We had no money for extras. Malcolm mowed lawns, blew leaves, shoveled snow to make money to pay for chess club two days after school. He was a good saver, some for basketball camp, some for college. Marcus, however, was having trouble adjusting to our new economic status. He cried when I told him we'd have to rent a saxophone for his lessons rather than buy him one. I cried, too, but alone, after they'd gone to bed. I sat in my living room, which was now family room, den and playroom combined, feeling sorry for myself. It had been a while since I'd let these feelings in. I'd actually thought I had put our swim club life behind me and moved seamlessly forward, virtuous in my new no-money position. Weren't people with money a little untrustworthy, a little less pure? Never having to think about how much the grocery bill is or feeding guests who dropped by unannounced or not buying a sweater because it has to be dry-cleaned. There were a hundred little things that made one's life different because of money and I hated having to think about them even more than I hated now not having money. When I didn't have a nanny before it was because I couldn't find a good one, even though everyone around me raved about their great help—nannies who treated the little darlings like they were their own. It doesn't work so straightforwardly brown on brown—there's resentment and tension and a mess of other crap. I finally said who needs it, I can take care of my own kids. It grew to be a matter of principle—but now I simply couldn't afford one. Now whenever I do need someone, I ask my dad, who has always been more than willing to help out. Our big old house said, *we are somebody, pay attention to us;* what does the new small house say? Christmas was coming and I'd have to get creative with the giving and right after that I'd have to start looking at camps. We wouldn't be able to afford Camp Minisink this year and I'd even have to start socking away for Y day camp. Malcolm was probably old enough to be a junior counselor.

Thinking about being broke, being poor, made me think about running into Gigi, a girl I knew from the community center where Mama used to teach and from one of my stints in public school. I'd had to give up shopping at Grant's and go to the grocery store that offered double coupons. As I stood in line behind her in the supermarket,

I'd recognized the side view but got distracted calculating the cost of the food I was putting on the conveyor belt.

"Ina, is that you, girl?"

Of course as soon as she said my name, it all came back. She had been the tiniest of the cheerleaders and she'd had an onion and big cheeks and big, high breasts. She had had a baby by a boy in high school.

"My son's twenty-one, he doin' good. Workin' for UPS. I got two grandkids. *Mmm.* What you doin' now? I heard you got a big-ass house, up the hill."

I began to space out, hearing her high-pitched voice, her words coming at me like a locomotive but I'm back at high school, seeing them together, Gigi and her quarterback; remembering her face flushed with the intensity of first love. I remember the rumor that they were going to get married right after high school. Then there was another rumor, that she'd let him have her onion. And another one, that he'd thrown her away like yesterday's beer bottle, not even recycled, just tossed in the trash to be tied up and carted out with everything else for raccoons to dig through.

Gigi continued like a nonstop train, not stopping even to take a breath as she ran down a list of names from high school, who had had a baby by whom, all were disconnects, and I was as far removed from them as the moon. Our community, our town, our people: what had happened? These girls had had babies with about as much thought as women I now know used to buy shoes. But what were our choices? Did any of us really have them? To be a baby's mama, driving a Lexus and living with your mama; to be some money-grubbing, social-climbing white-identified Negro? Are those the choices? How can you find yourself in a culture that tells you that you have to conform?

There are throngs of black folks running away from the Gigis who raised their babies on WIC, who believe working for UPS is great, who buy gold jewelry on layaway. Folks who distance themselves in all kinds of ways: *I'm not really black, I'm Indian, biracial, Hispanic . . . I'm from an upper-middle-class family; my great-grandfather was a physician; We've been going to the Vineyard, Sag Harbor, Idelwilde, since the forties; I went to Hahvad . . .* fill in the fucking blank. When did it become impossible to just be regular black? It made my head hurt.

"Ina, you alright?"

Gigi and the checkout boy were staring at me.

"Oh, I'm sorry, I just spaced . . ."

"That's alright. Listen, here's my number." She'd scribbled it on a magazine subscription card.

"Call me sometimes. We can catch up. You look like you could use a sister-friend from back in the day."

With that, she efficiently hooked her bag over her shoulder and pushed her cart out of the supermarket.

I took the number and folded it in half. I knew and even Rashid, the checkout boy, knew I'd never use it. I was touched, however weirdly, by her perceptive offer to talk. I did need help processing my old life and the new, my past and the future, but even with no cash, my life was still vastly different from the Gigis—not better or worse, just different, and the bridge was too prodigious to be crossed

now. I didn't tell her that I have a baby, probably the age
of one of her grandkids. She'd survived having been left
alone with her young son—she didn't mention the child's
father and she didn't have to. I knew she carried her own
water—and she wasn't crushed by it. Or was I just roman-
ticizing? Maybe the bridge wasn't that wide.

CHAPTER TWENTY-EIGHT

Thanksgiving used to be my favorite holiday, but this year was the second that I just couldn't get into it. I didn't want to cook, shop or have people over as had been part of our tradition for the last decade. It had been a year and two months since we separated and Jay and I were on friendly terms, enough for him to want to come for dinner and me to consider it. But as the days got closer, my mood got darker and I was just pissed off. I got a free turkey with bonus points from my new supermarket. No fresh free-range one delivered to my backdoor as in my other life. This one was frozen—would take two days to thaw, a hormone-injected basic turkey. I cut it out of the bag and it slipped across the tile counter, banging into the backsplash with a thud. I hated the way the cold felt against my hand. I punched it and my knuckle turned red. I put my fingers to my mouth and ran my tongue over them to feel warm. I pushed the turkey off the counter onto the floor, another louder thud on the ugly Mexican tile. I hated this tile—the grout, in someone else's lifetime, had been beige or cream but was now a cement color. It looked dead. The cabinets were a wooden, chestnut color that again at some earlier point in another century had been wonderful but now needed to be replaced; the yellow-and-white backsplash, the same. The gingham curtains I'd hung to try and give the kitchen a French country air were as charming as makeup on a pug. Who was I trying to fool? This house, this new life was not noble; I didn't feel any more alive without the anchors of all that materialism, I still felt adrift, alone, confused. Was I better than a year ago? Absolutely. Was I well? Hardly. It was angry time, when my moods took over and my mind raced and I couldn't think of anything good and wept a lot like I used to when Malcolm was little. I'd put him down to read to him for an hour until he asked me to stop. I'd loved to get lost in those childhood stories about homesick dogs and gorillas who go to school and a girl whose whole body turned to stripes because she was ashamed of liking lima beans. I'd cry when I read to him because I couldn't ever remember being read to by my mother when I was a child. My mother, who the neighbors thought was mother of the year, was always on her way to somewhere else. Malcolm would wipe the tears with the sleeve of his flannel pajama top and say:

"Mommy sad. Malcolm sad."

I'd kiss his sweet forehead and turn out his Winnie the Pooh lamp. He'd never fail to call me just as I'd hit the doorway.

"I tursty."

I'd get him water and rub his back while he drank.

"Good night again," we'd both say.

I'd crawl into my bed, still wearing my blouse and skirt from work; I'd thumb through some mindless magazines until I fell asleep. This was how I used to spend every night when Jay was building his business. I'd cook Malcolm frozen peas or corn or broccoli with fish sticks or chicken nuggets; cheese and crackers and a salad for me. Jay always ate at the office.

Now I was standing in this sorry kitchen, ruminating over conversations we'd had years ago: Jay looking at my series of self-portraits and asking what was the point. Years later he explained that he thought that I should show them in some formal way, that they were that good.

Oh, fuck him, what does he know? was what I thought at the time.

He knows how to make a buck. Or he used to.

I got on the phone to Marina. I needed to make some more money and I needed to work—shoot more. Her answer, which I knew before she'd said it, but didn't want to believe myself: Do weddings. I'd shot weddings as an assistant. I'd taken a course on hand-painting black-and-white photographs, which was a technique that made pictures look a little like old color paintings. I decided to offer it as a wedding portrait service. Marina agreed it was a great idea and it was good, fairly fast money.

I got one of the kids from the gallery to help me make a brochure and I made up business cards, calling myself Ina West, dropping Jay's last name. I worked overtime at the paper to make the money I needed to do a mailing and take out an ad in the local paper. My appeal was the color painting and I was cheap. "Stress the cheap part," Kayreen had advised. When my ad ran, I got several jobs that would take me through till the new year.

The first clients I got through a mother of the bride who knew Jay from high school. Rachel and Steve, a couple who'd just graduated from Oberlin—kids. No one born in the early eighties should be allowed to get married; but that wasn't what they hired me for. They wanted me to capture their beauty—which was obvious; and their love—who can see that? The beauty part was easy. She had glistening skin like the color of a Dove Bar; she had a large mouth, a small nose, swimmer's shoulders and per-fect hands. She and Steve, who had loose brownish-blond twizzle-curls that he wore pulled back and tied with a piece of rawhide, they were both long and thin with torsos that seemed to dance. They finished each other's sen-tences, sat close and had a similar delicate way. I first met with them at Rachel's parents' house to talk about what they wanted.

"It's going to be a small, holiday wedding," Rachel said, her voice a little-girl whisper.

"But it's not holiday-themed," Steve inserted, with his soft voice.

"Right, right, no red and green. More like a winter won-derland," she said, slipping her hand from his to motion her point.

I looked at these two; ebony-and-ivory matched sets of Banana Republic perfection and tried to remember if I'd

ACTING OUT

ever been this young, felt like they do right now. Did we
finish each other's sentences? Hold hands on the couch?
Believe you needed to feel the other's touch in order to
breathe? I couldn't remember.

". . . really take advantage of the season, we're hoping it
snows," Steve said.

"And you know we want black and white, with the col-
oration you do?" Rachel asked.

"Yes, yes, I know that. It'll be beautiful, we'll be able to
get your skin tones just right."

I looked down into their entwined hands. I couldn't tell
whether I'd embarrassed her or what.

"Isn't it gorgeous," Steve said, more to her than me.

"Yes, beautiful. It's hard to get the tones right with
black and white when the skin tones are extreme," I said,
looking around, feeling like I just discovered I was at a
meeting of some kind of cult instead of a cocktail party.

"Yeah, that's why we called you. Your husband told my
mom that you could give us what we want," Rachel said.

My husband? It had been a while since I'd heard Jay
mentioned in that way.

"Yeah, so there're just a few things I need you to fill
out," I said, handing them my basic questionnaire. "And
I'll need a deposit."

Steve took the form and Rachel handed me a signed but
otherwise blank check.

"Um, Rachel, you didn't fill in the amount."

"Oh, you just tell us what you need. You can fill it out."

This really was a lucky day. Weddings are either the easiest or hardest money you'll ever make, Marina had said. It

all depends on the people. Rachel and Steve seemed to be firmly in the former.

On the day of their wedding it did snow, only a powdering, though, and by the time the event started the sun had come out; but the Pomona Garden Club had been transformed into a winter wonderland, just as they'd wanted. Fake trees had been covered in fake snow; white felt, white cotton fluffs on the chairs for the guests, the altar, everything. All the guests wore winter white. Everyone on the bride's side was beautiful—the clothes, the hair, makeup, manners, all impeccable. Steve's parents looked like models from a Brooks Brothers catalog, but the rest of his side were decidedly B-flat white folks in Spiegel wear. I was in my professional outfit—black pants, black V-neck and red loafers, needless to say, I stood out but it didn't matter. I was there to capture this ideal couple—perfect subjects who didn't raise their voices, didn't snap, didn't respond sarcastically, nothing. I was concerned for them. Who were these people? Me, I didn't fit in and, for the first time since I can remember, I liked it. I am an artist, someone who feels every single thing, who can't and won't pretend anymore. Isn't that a life worth having, not pretending anymore.

I drove home thinking about Rachel and Steve's future. She ladylike and chic and he a hip white guy, so cool he would coparent to the point of maybe being a stay-at-home dad. She would teach something like art or music to private school first-graders and they'd spend their summers in places like Nantucket and Tuscany, the Adirondacks or Montpelier. Rachel's mother had planned for poor Rachel before she was even conceived, now she just had to live it out, so she could get it over with and finally get to her own life. But would she? In a way her life had been like mine—everything had come too easily. Was it glamorous enough? How long would it take her to want more than that? I peered carefully through my windshield, which was smeared with remnants of the day's snow and dirt. I felt joy and sadness for what I had gone through, realizing that I had traveled Rachel's road before I got to do my own thing. It's so much easier, initially, to just wear the clothes that your mother has laid out for you.

Early in our marriage, around our fifth anniversary Jay and I had gone to couple's counseling. We'd decided to after coming back from a trip we had taken to try to get back to each other—his idea—to start having regular sex again. We'd gotten one of those Valentine's Day packages at a couple's resort. The Kingston airport had been small, hot and cramped. The dancers that met incoming tourists swirled in red, yellow and white outfits with matching scarves. It was supposed to be joyous, but they were so clearly not; I didn't feel uplifted. The natives were singing and dancing but there was an all-business quality in their eyes, no joy. A woman offered cups of warm, red, overly sweet punch to the newly arrived. Welcome to Jamaica, she said. The country was poor then, but it's even worse now. An American dollar is about twenty to their one. And their dollar value continues to drop. I couldn't enjoy myself among those facts.

On the trip, Jay and I went through the motions: we would lie on the beach, go shopping at the resort and into one of the hill-town outdoor bazaars, eat too much, drink lots of rum punch. Jay had barely been speaking to me by the time we got back from the vacation. Being away from home simply highlighted our problems. We didn't enjoy the same things: he liked parasailing and scuba diving and dancing in the disco until it closed. I liked reading on the beach, taking long walks and riding the hotel bike. We each found the other boring. We didn't even have sex after the first night. That was how I finally convinced Jay that we needed to see a therapist. He agreed to go only if I found a black, male therapist with a Ph.D. I did and we did.

"So tell me why you're here," Brotherman therapist began, and looked at Jay and then me.

Jay mumbled something about our vacation, how we were so different, how we weren't getting along.

The therapist turned to me and said my name. As if to tell me it was my turn to talk now and I could stop arguing with Jay in my mind.

He was an average-size man, maybe five foot eleven, medium build, no facial hair, everything about him was average except he had enormous feet, must have worn a size fifteen. I sat there, looking at his size-fifteen brown wing tips, thinking about what he was thinking, seeing. Who did he see before him and which of our stories would he believe?

"We went on vacation and didn't have a great time," I said distractedly.

Jay jumped in. "Now I'll be the first to admit I'm not the

easiest person to get along with, I have my opinions and ways of doing things and I may not be the most stimulating person who ever lived, but I love my wife and my kids and take care of them. Maybe I could listen to Ina more, but after a while she just says the same thing over and over. That gets tiresome, especially after a hard week. Okay, maybe I could be more open to going to some of those different kinds of restaurants Ina likes, Moroccan and Vietnamese and what have you. Maybe I should go with her to the museums and galleries, but I'm busy building a business. Real estate is like a baby—it's nonstop. When the business is booming you're busy seven days, when it's not you're trying to drum up business every day."

"Tell me about your parents, Jay."

Jay stopped, as if he were a stalled battery.

He took a couple of breaths and continued.

"My background didn't prepare me for anything that I'm living now. Mom and Dad split before I ever remembered them together. My moms worked all the time, double shifts at the post office. Me and my brother stayed with whatever neighbor or relative was around. Somebody was always willing to baby-sit. My moms did her best, don't get me wrong, but a woman can't raise a man."

He inhaled again, letting out air, letting us know this was difficult for him.

"And Ina's family, whoa, those folks is wack."

"Leave my family out of it," I said.

"Yes, Jay, let's stay on your family."

He nodded; knowing his attempt to change the subject had been poor.

"My dad, man, I used to think he was a hero. When he showed up with his big arms, he would pick both of us up, and he had all this energy. He'd take me and my brother for the day, Saturdays usually. We'd just go to the park and out for burgers, but it was the best time in my life, just leaving my moms for a while, who was always so down, so tired. She was a victim and I wasn't going to be one, I didn't even want to be around that. I swore I'd never leave my kids, though. It was one thing, as I got older, that I had to give to her. She hung in there. She did what she had to do to raise us. My dad booked. As much as I loved him, I didn't respect that."

Jay started to tear up. Brotherman therapist handed him a box of tissues, which Jay took.

He sat quiet for a moment and sniffed his tears back, composed himself before he started talking again.

"I just wanted a dad."

I felt for Jay. We'd never had this conversation before. I reached over and patted his knee.

Jay let go now, as if my patting him was encouraging him to cry. He heaved and sighed and let it out. I'd never seen him like this.

After he quieted down, the therapist looked at me and asked me why I thought we were sitting here.

"Well, my life is something I've been doing with my eyes shut and I'm tired of hearing myself complaining. My mind is just a fog, my limbs hurt and I just drag myself through my days.

"When I was a little girl I fantasized that I would grow up and have a beautiful house and children and a husband who I loved. It seemed so simple, as things do, I

ACTING OUT

guess, when you're a child. Now I look around and that's pretty much what I have and there's no happiness anywhere around. I wonder what went wrong with my fantasy."

"Tell me about how you met?"

Jay told him the basics.

"We met at college, but we didn't really know each other. I was in a fraternity and Ina was anti all that. I was attracted to her, who wouldn't be, but she wasn't my type, at least back then she wasn't."

"Your type?"

"Yeah, you know, I was going out with the kind of women who went to college to find a husband—girlie types, long hair, dressed up. Ina was the opposite of that." Jay smiled and looked at me.

I didn't smile back.

I'm sure I got a demerit from the therapist for that.

"Go on, Jay."

"Well, I ran into Ina after we graduated and we went out a few times and we had a good time, I thought, but then she kinda disappeared and then I ran into her again, in the city when I was in grad school and she was working as a photographer . . ."

"An assistant," I interrupted.

"A photographer's assistant and we started hanging out again and this time we got serious and she got pregnant and we got married."

"Were you planning on getting married before she got pregnant?"

"Oh yeah," Jay said, quickly.

"No," I said.

He looked at both of us again, this time with a bemused expression.

"So who wants to go first?" he asked.

Jay motioned his hand as if to say, *after you.*

"We hadn't talked about marriage. We were living together. Jay and I used to get along well and it was easy between us, but we weren't talking about marriage—"

"Well, Ina, that's what people do, usually . . ." Jay interrupted.

"Oh really, Jay, and where's that written?"

"You . . ." he waved his hand at me and I stopped talking.

"Now Ina wants to rewrite our story and naturally she wants to make me the bad guy, or at least the guy who never got it. I know exactly who Ina is; she's the one who's confused. There aren't many things that confuse me, people don't. I can tell who someone is in minutes. She was a confused little girl when we got married. She wanted a family, she didn't have much of one growing up and I gave that to her. Everything she ever wanted I gave to her. Now she says that I don't get it; I don't know her. Bullshit. She's just bored now and looking for somebody to blame. I've been telling her ever since she stopped working with me that she needed a job, a hobby, something. I know the type of person she is would never be satisfied with all those activities that fill up time. It's not her. I encouraged her to go to art school; I fixed up the room in the basement, made it into a dark room . . . ."

"That's not how I remember it," I said.

"And how's that?"

"*I* fixed up the dark room . . ."

"Okay, Ina, but who suggested it and paid for it?"

I didn't say anything. I crossed my arms.

"I just wanted her to find something outside the house that was hers, that she could be proud of—photography, beading, any damn thing. Does that sound like somebody who doesn't get it? I knew she needed to do her art and that was one of the things that attracted me to her at Howard, albeit from afar. She was doing her own thing and that really turned me on."

"Do you use the dark room?" Brotherman asked.

Jay looked at me, knowing the answer, but somehow needing to witness my humiliation.

"No, I don't."

We got deeper in during the sessions that followed and I began to feel less like Brotherman and Jay were on the same team opposite me. In one, when we began describing our years before we got married, I finally told them the thing I'd never told anyone.

"I got raped," I whispered.

Both Brotherman therapist and Jay sat up in their chairs.

"You what?" Jay said, looking at the floor, but turned toward me. "When? What are you talking about?"

It was the first time I'd ever said it out loud and it felt amazingly good. I felt calm, a little shaky, but not afraid like I'd always thought I would've been reliving that time. Saying it finally put it in a bearable form.

"I was raped when I was working for Corey, it was one of his friends."

Neither of them spoke.

"That was when I moved into your apartment."

Jay rubbed his forehead with his index finger. Brotherman therapist sat back in his swivel chair and looked at me.

"I've never told anyone. I somehow felt it was my fault."

"Why'd you feel that?" the therapist asked.

"'Cause I'd let him stay over. He asked if he could sleep on the couch so he didn't have to wake up his roommate and I believed him and . . ."

"But why'd you keep it from me?" Jay asked.

I looked at him, and the concern in his eyes made me want to try harder at making our marriage work.

"I don't know."

After several more sessions, hashing out who did what and how, Brotherman released us with exercises. We were to talk uninterrupted for ten minutes each day. We were to write down every time one of us made the other crazy/angry/resentful and we were to come back in three months. We did the exercises for two months.

We never went back.

CHAPTER TWENTY-NINE

I now have a dark room in a hall closet. The one I used to have, the one that went unused, was three times this size with an outer room for shelving space, a cutter and a drafting table. Is it true that one must struggle for something in order to appreciate it?

I had done six weddings in three months and was exhausted, but my bank account was getting padded and I was content. Jay was working at combining the residential and commercial sides of his business. Our children were being shuttled and rushed between us and I knew they weren't each doing fine, but I needed them to hold on until I could get past this busy phase. Kids, unfortunately, don't work like that.

I'd spent the first half of my life trying to be happy wearing someone else's clothes; the second would be living by my own definition. Successful living varies as much

as people; for some it is to be considered beautiful or having connections or the great job or house or wardrobe or
rich parents or peace of mind or, for me, a contented soul.
Sometimes that contentment comes by just cleaning out
your nose or your closet or having your begonias bloom
just right or giving a friend the perfect birthday present.
It's dinners with friends that linger till past 2:00 A.M. and
you had no idea it was so late.

The principal was the lovely man who bought my first
photograph. God's grace, I whispered to myself as Jay and
I sat waiting in his office to hear about why Marcus was
getting suspended. He'd had two previous arguments, two
warnings, and this time he'd hit a boy with a tray, across
the boy's face.

"It was very aggressive," the principal said. "And of
course you know about his refusal to do his homework?"

We nodded.

"Has Marcus ever been in therapy? Are there some issues at home that might be making him so angry?"

We told him about the separation, the moving, without
going into details.

He nodded with his eyes half-closed, indicating that he
understood; saw this kind of thing all the time.

"Listen. I know he's a good kid; he's very bright. Why
don't you take him for a few days, just be with him, listen
to him . . ."

"We've been doing that," Jay said, not hiding the anger
in his voice.

"Well, Mr. Robinson, I guess you're going to have to do it some more."

"I think he needs more than listening," Jay said.

The principal didn't respond.

I thanked him for his time and told him that we'd work things out with Marcus.

We walked out of the principal's office into the larger room, which was the school office, and saw Marcus sitting on a hard wooden bench, head down, forcefully swinging his spindly legs back and forth. Jay and I walked over to him and Jay hissed through his teeth. "Get up."

Marcus looked up with fear in his eyes.

"Let's go," Jay said, walking behind Marcus.

I touched Jay's arm, letting him know he needed to lighten up.

"Get in the car," Jay said, holding open the door to his car.

I stood outside the car, speaking to Jay over the car's roof.

"I know you're pissed, but this isn't the way to handle him now."

"Oh yeah, Ina, and what do you think we should do? Give him a party?"

"I think we should decide what to do first, before talking to him, that's all."

Jay paused before getting into the car and reluctantly agreed.

We got back to my house and told Marcus to go to his room. I put on a pot for coffee and Jay and I sat facing each other at the kitchen table.

"So?"

"So," I said. "He's clearly in pain over all that's happening with us. We shouldn't punish him for that."

"Well, what should we do?"

He'd never deferred to me so plaintively.

"I think you should spend some one-on-one time with him. I think we should tell him our plans, make him know that his world won't change drastically, no more than it already has."

I got up and poured coffee into two mugs and sat them both on the table between us. Jay poured cream and too much sugar into his and took a sip.

"Ina, I don't want a divorce."

"Where'd that come from?"

"I've been wanting to say it, ever since last Christmas—"

"Last Christmas," I interrupted.

"Yes, when she showed up. It was clear to me then that I'd fucked up . . ."

"So why didn't you just say that then? You've waited practically a year."

"We'd been just going through the motions, you know that. It was all about the kids, the house. You had already checked out long before I left."

"Maybe, but we were together, in the same house. Our kids weren't suffering."

Jay looked contrite.

"I feel like shit. I know this is all my fault. I never wanted to hurt my kids. I swore I never would . . ."

"But it happened. Look, he'll be all right."

"But what about us?"

"What about us?" I said, taking a sip. "You left me for another woman."

"I was so lonely."

"Lonely? What are you talking about? How could you have possibly been lonely?"

"Ina, you weren't . . ."

"I was always here. Don't even try to blame this shit on me."

"No, I'm not looking to blame, I'm just saying, we drifted apart. It was all about the kids and the lessons, the house . . ."

"You wanted all of this, remember?"

"I did, and I do. We just stopped having fun."

"And now, just like that, you want it all back." I got up from the table and walked to the counter, leaning against the sink.

"I don't know, Jay. I don't know if I want you back." I looked at Jay who looked like he'd just been smacked. Surely he didn't think it would be that easy. *I wanna come home* and I'd just say okay.

"Ina, this was never about somebody else."

"You didn't think that then."

"No, I probably did think that I wanted someone else. But I know now I don't."

I took a drink of my coffee, which had gotten cold. I was too stimulated now for coffee anyway. I looked over at Jay, who was sitting before me looking like a dog at the pound who wanted nothing more than to be taken home.

"I don't know, Jay. We've got to figure out what to do about Marcus."

He nodded and finished his coffee. "I know this is kind

of sudden. You don't have to respond now. I just wanted you to know what I've been thinking and seeing you take over and get your work going and all, I'm really glad for you. It's like you've become the person I fell I love with."

"Mom," Marcus called from the top of the stairs. "Can I come down now?"

"No," Jay and I said in unison.

We looked at each other and grinned.

"I'll go up," he said.

"Be gentle."

He got up to make his way upstairs but turned to me. "I have an idea."

Jay took Malcolm to his brother's house in Pennsylvania, in the Poconos for the three days of his suspension. His brother would be at the firehouse in Pomona, working a few double shifts, and so they'd have the house to themselves. All that hiking and chopping wood and being outside would be good for him. They could talk without distractions. We'd visited Jay's brother only twice, once when he and his wife bought the place and once after she'd moved out, taking all the furniture with her. It was a newly developed area, with good-sized homes at affordable prices, in a place that was previously woods, now repackaged into commuter communities for working people looking for suburban sprawl, which was increasingly farther to reach. Other than woods, strip and outlet malls there was nothing there. It was a perfect place to talk.

Jay needed to listen to Marcus as much as Marcus needed to be with him. Their temperaments were the same, but where Jay had had to strive, Marcus had had things handed to him, which was why Jay was so angry at him for screwing up in school.

"Man, you have everything, but you still can't afford to fuck up. We don't have it like that."

Marcus didn't understand what his father was talking about but when Marcus told Malcolm—who had told me—he, as the big brother, was able to interpret. "Dad was poor, his dad wasn't around, they had to struggle. He thinks it's still the old days."

The old days were how our kids referred to anytime before they were born. They believed the world was integrated and free and fair because for the most part that was their world, what they had experienced. It was past time for us to explain to them that while their lives seemed free of prejudice it wasn't, and that some people would still judge them negatively because they were black, because some people were ignorant. Marcus got his talk during their stay in the Poconos. It wasn't something either of us had looked forward to, but we both knew they had to be told. We'd debated for years whether to tell them what we knew or to let them find out on their own. Suppose they didn't get slapped; suppose they did skate through, free to be who they were. Why should we introduce such if it hadn't touched them? We spent years arguing this and doing nothing. When Marcus got into trouble, we knew, while he was wrong, he had to understand that there were things he wouldn't be able to get away with, that he'd always be held to a different standard because he was a black boy first, an individual second. "But that's not fair, I'm *Marcus*," he'd say. You're right, it's not, but that's how it is.

CHAPTER THIRTY

"So are you going to homecoming?"

"Nah. Can't really get away, too much going on at the community center, at the office."

"I can't believe you're not going."

Jay sprinkled hot sauce on his omelet.

"I wanna stay close to home, especially when you have to travel."

I looked back down at the newspaper I'd been scanning. I had to pack for my first out-of-town shoot. A couple had read about my color-printed wedding photos and was flying me to Atlanta to shoot their wedding. I had another in D.C. and then Chicago after that. And I was getting paid for it. I couldn't believe my life.

"Oh, I have something for you." I got up from the table.

"For me?"

I went into my basement study and pulled the photo of Jay I'd taken when he was in a Step Show at Howard.

"Do you remember?" I said, handing the frame to him.

He looked at it as if it were some long-lost artifact.

"Oh man. This is great. Look at Boo and Charlie. Is that Hank in the background . . . ?"

He was asking but he knew the answers. He knew who they were and he relished looking at his old friends, his brothers, his lost youth. He looked at me, still beaming. "Thank you."

"You're welcome. I finally found it and then got it framed. I've been meaning to give it to you since we moved into this house."

He looked down again, staring at it, like he couldn't believe what he saw.

"You know I remember this night like it was last week."

"Those were the best days, huh?"

"They were good, but no, not the best. These are the best days."

I looked at Jay, who looked back at me with an aching love in his eyes.

"What?"

"I was just thinking what if I hadn't gone to that club that night?"

"What club? What're you talking about?"

"Kenya Club."

I laughed out loud at the thought of the place where we'd remet after college.

"We probably wouldn't have gotten together."

What if? What if my mother had been a successful

artist? What if she'd supported my artistic dreams? What if I hadn't gotten raped? What if the Harlem business had been a big success? What if? There are hundreds of them, ways life coulda turned out different based on one different decision, direction, piece of advice.

"What if we hadn't been at that club? I have no idea what would've happened. I only know what did."

"Are you glad you did?" His eyes were begging for an answer he could live with.

I reached across the table and lightly touched his face with the side of my hand.

"Look at what we made together."

As I felt his whiskers touch the back of my hand, I knew we would never be as we were. Our innocence was gone. We'd broken our vows to each other. What I had now was what you always have: a choice. I could be pissed at him forever and blame him for screwing up the perfect image on the Christmas card. I could be suspicious every time I couldn't find him, or I could thank him for forcing me to find the person that had been missing for a long time.

Jay smiled, and I smiled back at him, seeing the same picture in my head that he held in his. Our relationship wasn't the same and for that we were both grateful, even though getting to this place had caused our family so much pain. We had made something amazing and no matter how we got here, we were here, two wholes sealed together—imperfections and all.

BENILDE LITTLE is the bestselling author of *Good Hair* and *The Itch*. A graduate of Howard University, she has been a reporter at the *Newark Star-Ledger*, *People Magazine*, and an editor at *Essence*. She lives in New Jersey with her husband and two young children.